University of Londo... - 6 JUL 2017 2 7 DEC 20
Naval Volunteer Reserve. H..................... and
his work as a language teacher took ...... over the
world. Clive King has attempted to learn ten
languages, including Tamil, Bengali, Gaelic and
Anglo-Saxon. He has not been incredibly successful
with any of them, but many of his stories deal with
language difficulties of one sort or another.

Clive King comes from a family of DIY fanatics.
In his home you can see such things as a homemade
built-in ironing board, a panelled kitchen and an oak
staircase. He lives with his family in Norfolk and is a
full-time writer.

CLIVE KING

Stig of the Dump

Illustrated by Edward Ardizzono

PUFFIN

For C. J. K.

PUFFIN BOOKS

Published by the Penguin Group
Penguin Books Ltd, 80 Strand, London WC2R ORL, England
Penguin Group (USA) Inc., 375 Hudson Street, New York, New York 10014, USA
Penguin Group (Canada), 90 Eglinton Avenue East, Suite 700, Toronto, Ontario, Canada M4P 2Y3
(a division of Pearson Penguin Canada Inc.)
Penguin Ireland, 25 St Stephen's Green, Dublin 2, Ireland (a division of Penguin Books Ltd)
Penguin Group (Australia), 707 Collins Street, Melbourne, Victoria 3008, Australia (a division of Pearson Australia Group Pty Ltd)
Penguin Books India Pvt Ltd, 11 Community Centre, Panchsheel Park, New Delhi – 110 017, India
Penguin Group (NZ), 67 Apollo Drive, Rosedale, Auckland 0632, New Zealand
(a division of Pearson New Zealand Ltd)
Penguin Books (South Africa) (Pty) Ltd, Block D, Rosebank Office Park, 181 Jan Smuts Avenue,
Parktown North, Gauteng 2193, South Africa

Penguin Books Ltd, Registered Offices: 80 Strand, London WC2R ORL, England

puffinbooks.com

First published 1963
This edition published 2013
002

Text copyright © Clive King, 1963
Illustrations by Edward Ardizzone
All rights reserved

The moral right of the author and illustrator has been asserted

Filmset in Linotype Baskerville
Printed in Great Britain by Clays Ltd, St Ives plc

British Library Cataloguing in Publication Data
A CIP catalogue record for this book is available from the British Library

ISBN: 978-0-141-34875-9

www.greenpenguin.co.uk

Contents

1. The Ground Gives Way

IF you went too near the edge of the chalk-pit the ground would give way. Barney had been told this often enough. Everybody had told him. His grandmother, every time he came to stay with her. His sister, every time she wasn't telling him something else. Barney had a feeling, somewhere in his middle, that it was probably true about the ground giving way. But still, there was a difference between being told and seeing it happen. And today was one of those grey days when there was nothing to do, nothing to play, and nowhere to go. Except to the chalk-pit. The dump.

Barney got through the rickety fence and went to the

7

edge of the pit. This had been the side of a hill once, he told himself. Men had come to dig away chalk and left this huge hole in the earth. He thought of all the sticks of chalk they must have made, and all the blackboards in all the schools they must have written on. They must have dug and dug for hundreds of years. And then they got tired of digging, or somebody had told them to stop before they dug away all the hill. And now they did not know what to do with this empty hole and they were trying to fill it up again. Anything people didn't want they threw into the bottom of the pit.

He crawled through the rough grass and peered over. The sides of the pit were white chalk, with lines of flints poking out like bones in places. At the top was crumbly brown earth and the roots of the trees that grew on the edge. The roots looped over the edge, twined in the air and grew back into the earth. Some of the trees hung over the edge, holding on desperately by a few roots. The earth and chalk had fallen away beneath them, and one day they too would fall to the bottom of the pit. Strings of ivy and the creeper called Old Man's Beard hung in the air.

Far below was the bottom of the pit. The dump. Barney could see strange bits of wreckage among the moss and elder bushes and nettles. Was that the steering wheel of a ship? The tail of an aeroplane? At least there was a real bicycle. Barney felt sure he could make it go if only he could get at it. They didn't let him have a bicycle.

Barney wished he was at the bottom of the pit.

And the ground gave way.

Barney felt his head going down and his feet going up. There was a rattle of falling earth beneath him. Then he was falling, still clutching the clump of grass that was falling with him.

'This is what it's like when the ground gives way,' thought Barney. Then he seemed to turn a complete somersault in the air, bumped into a ledge of chalk half-way down, crashed through some creepers and ivy and branches, and landed on a bank of moss.

His thoughts did those funny things they do when you bump your head and you suddenly find yourself thinking about what you had for dinner last Tuesday, all mixed up with seven times six. Barney lay with his eyes shut, waiting for his thoughts to stop being mixed up. Then he opened them.

He was lying in a kind of shelter. Looking up he could see a roof, or part of a roof, made of elder branches, a very rotten old carpet, and rusty old sheets of iron. There was a big hole, through which he must have fallen. He could see the white walls of the cliff, the trees and creepers at the top, and the sky with clouds passing over it.

Barney decided he wasn't dead. He didn't even seem to be very much hurt. He turned his head and looked around him. It was dark in this den after looking at the white chalk, and he couldn't see what sort of a place it was. It seemed to be partly a cave dug into the chalk, partly a shelter built out over the mouth of the cave. There was a cool, damp smell. Woodlice and earwigs dropped from the roof where he had broken through it.

But what had happened to his legs? He couldn't sit

up when he tried to. His legs wouldn't move. Perhaps I've broken them, Barney thought. What shall I do then? He looked at his legs to see if they were all right, and found they were all tangled up with creeper from the face of the cliff. Who tied me up? thought Barney. He kicked his legs to try to get them free, but it was no use, there were yards of creeper trailing down from the cliff. I suppose I got tangled up when I fell, he thought. Expect I would have broken my neck if I hadn't.

He lay quiet and looked around the cave again. Now that his eyes were used to it he could see further into the dark part of the cave.

There was somebody there!

Or Something!

*

Something, or Somebody, had a lot of shaggy black hair and two bright black eyes that were looking very hard at Barney.

'Hullo!' said Barney.

Something said nothing.

'I fell down the cliff,' said Barney.

Somebody grunted.

'My name's Barney.'

Somebody-Something made a noise that sounded like 'Stig'.

'D'you think you could help me undo my feet, Mr Stig?' asked Barney politely. 'I've got a pocket-knife,' he added, remembering that he had in his pocket a knife he'd found among the wood-shavings on the floor of Grandfather's workshop. It was quite a good knife except that one blade had come off and the other one was broken in half and rather blunt.

'Good thing I put it in my pocket,' he thought. He wriggled so he could reach the knife, and managed to open the rusty half-blade. He tried to reach the creepers round his legs, but found it was difficult to cut creepers with a blunt knife when your feet are tied above your head.

The Thing sitting in the corner seemed to be interested. It got up and moved towards Barney into the light. Barney was glad to see it was Somebody after all. 'Funny way to dress though,' he thought, 'rabbit skins round the middle and no shoes or socks.'

'Oh puff!' said Barney, 'I can't reach my feet. You do it, Stig!'

He handed the knife to Stig.

Stig turned it over and felt it with his strong hairy hands, and tested the edge with a thumb. Then instead of trying to cut the creepers he squatted down on the ground and picked up a broken stone.

He's going to sharpen the knife, thought Barney.

But no, it seemed more as if he was sharpening the stone. Using the hard knife to chip with, Stig was carefully flaking tiny splinters off the edge of the flint, until he had a thin sharp blade. Then he sprang up, and with two or three slashes cut through the creeper that tied Barney's feet.

Barney sat up. 'Golly!' he said. 'You *are* clever! I bet my Grandad couldn't do that, and he's *very* good at making things.'

Stig grinned. Then he went to the back of the cave and hid the broken knife under a pile of rubbish.

'My knife!' protested Barney. But Stig took no
notice. Barney got up and went into the dark part of
the cave.

He'd never seen anything like the collection of bits
and pieces, odds and ends, bric-à-brac and old brock,
that this Stig creature had lying about his den. There
were stones and bones, fossils and bottles, skins and

tins, stacks of sticks and hanks of string. There were
motor-car tyres and hats from old scarecrows, nuts and
bolts and bobbles from brass bedsteads. There was a
coal scuttle full of dead electric light bulbs and a basin
with rusty screws and nails in it. There was a pile of
bracken and newspapers that looked as if it were used
for a bed. The place looked as if it had never been
given a tidy-up.

'I wish I lived here,' said Barney.

Stig seemed to understand that Barney was approving of his home and his face lit up. He took on the air of a householder showing a visitor round his property, and began pointing out some of the things he seemed particularly proud of.

First, the plumbing. Where the water dripped through a crack in the roof of the cave he had wedged the mud-guard of a bicycle. The water ran along this, through the tube of a vacuum-cleaner, and into a big can with writing on it. By the side of this was a plastic football carefully cut in half, and Stig dipped up some water and offered it to Barney. Barney had swallowed a mouthful before he made out the writing on the can: it said WEEDKILLER. However, the water only tasted of rust and rubber.

It was dark in the back of the cave. Stig went to the front where the ashes of a fire were smoking faintly, blew on them, picked up a book that lay beside his bed, tore out a page and rolled it up, lit it at the fire, and carried it to a lamp set in a niche in the wall. As it flared up Barney could see it was in fact an old teapot, filled with some kind of oil, and with a bootlace hanging out of it for a wick.

In the light of the lamp Stig went to the very back of the cave and began to thump the wall and point, and explain something in his strange grunting language. Barney did not understand a word but he recognized the tone of voice – like when grown-ups go on about: 'I'm thinking of tearing this down, and building on here, and having this done up ...' Stig had been digging into the wall, enlarging his cave. There was a bit of an old bed he had been using as a pick, and a baby's bath full of loose chalk to be carried away.

Barney made the interested sort of noises you are supposed to make when people tell you they are going to put up plastic wallpaper with pictures of mouse-traps on it, but Stig reached up to a bunch of turnips hanging from a poker stuck in the wall. He handed Barney a turnip, took one for himself, and began to eat it. Barney sat down on a bundle of old magazines done up with string and munched the turnip. The turnip at least was fresh, and it tasted better to him than the cream of spinach he'd hidden under his spoon at dinner time.

Barney looked at Stig. Funny person to find living next door to you, he thought. Stig did not seem much bigger than himself, but he looked very strong and his hands looked cleverer than his face. But how old was he? Ten? Twenty? A hundred? A thousand?

'You been here long?' asked Barney.

Stig grinned again. 'Long,' he said. 'Long, long, long.' But it sounded more like an echo, or a parrot copying somebody, than an answer to his question.

'I'm staying at my Grandmother's house,' said Barney. Stig just looked at him. 'Oh well,' thought Barney, 'if he's not interested in talking I don't mind.' He stood up.

'I better go now,' he said. 'Thank you for having me. Can I have my knife back, please?'

Stig still looked blank.

'Knife,' said Barney, and made cutting movements with his hand. Stig picked up the sharp worked flint from the floor of the cave and gave it to Barney.

'Oo, can I have that!' exclaimed Barney. 'Thank you!'

He looked at the stone, hard and shiny, almost like a diamond and much more useful. Then he put it in his pocket, said good-bye again, and went out of the low door of the shelter.

It was getting late in the autumn evening, and it was already dark and gloomy in the pit. Barney knew there was a way out right at the other end of the pit, and by going a long way round he could get back to the house. There were rustlings in dry leaves and muffled sounds from the middle of bramble patches, but somehow Barney found he didn't mind. He felt the hard stone in his pocket and thought of Stig in his den under the cliff. You weren't likely to find anything stranger than Stig wherever you looked. And, well, Stig was his friend.

When he got back to the house his Grandmother and his sister Lou were just coming in from feeding the hens.

'Where have you been all the time?' asked his Grandmother.

'I went to the chalk pit,' said Barney.

'All by yourself!' exclaimed Lou.

'Yes, of course,' he said.

'What have you been doing?' his Grandmother asked.

'Well, I fell and bumped my head.'

'Poor old Barney!' said Lou, and laughed.

'But it was all right,' Barney went on. 'Because I met Stig.'

'Who's Stig?' they both asked together.

'He's a sort of boy,' replied Barney. 'He just wears rabbit skins and lives in a cave. He gets his water through a vacuum cleaner and puts chalk in his bath. He's my friend.'

'Good gracious!' exclaimed his Grandmother. 'What funny friends you have, dear!'

'He means he's been playing Cave Men,' Lou exclaimed helpfully. 'Stig's just a pretend-friend, isn't he, Barney?'

'No, he's really true!' Barney protested.

'Of course he's true,' his Grandmother smiled. 'Now, Lou. Don't tease Barney!'

'Let's pretend Stig's a wicked wizard who lives in a cave and turns people into stone,' Lou began eagerly. She was always inventing stories and games like that.

'No,' said Barney quietly, feeling the sharp flint in his pocket. 'Stig's nice. He's my friend.'

That night he kept the flint under his pillow, and thought of Stig out there in the pit sleeping on his bed of bracken and old newspapers. He wished he lived all the time at Granny's house so that he could get to know Stig. He had to go back the day after tomorrow. Never mind, he'd visit Stig in the morning.

2. Digging With Stig

It was a fine autumn morning and the grass was very
wet with dew outside. Barney pushed his breakfast
down as fast as he could manage.

'What do you want to do today?' his Grandmother
asked as she drank her coffee. 'I have to go in to Sevenoaks this morning. Do you want to come?'

Barney's heart sank. Go in to Sevenoaks? Well it
was all right if you had nothing else to do. But he had
to go and see Stig.

'No thank you, Granny,' he said. 'I don't think I
want to go in to Sevenoaks.'

'You'll be quite happy just messing about here?' asked his Grandmother.

'Yes thank you. I just want to mess about. With – with Stig.'

'Oh, I see,' Granny smiled. 'With your friend Stig. Well, Mrs Pratt will be here all the morning, so if you like you can stay with her. And with Stig, of course.'

Lou said she would like to go in to the town as she wasn't particularly interested in playing with Stig. Barney knew from the way she said it that she still thought Stig was only a pretend-friend. But that was all right. If she didn't want to meet Stig, she needn't.

'Can I go out now?' he asked.

'All right,' said Granny. 'Put your boots on!' she called after him as he shot through the door.

Barney's feet made dark prints in the dew as he headed across the lawn towards the chalk-pit. Then he stopped, and stood still in the middle of the lawn. Suppose he didn't find Stig after all?

The sun was bright. Yellow leaves fluttered down from the elm tree on to the grass. A robin puffed its breast on a rose tree and squeaked at him. Barney suddenly wasn't sure that he believed in Stig himself. It wasn't a Stiggish day, like yesterday when he had fallen down the pit.

He *had* fallen, hadn't he? He felt the bump on the back of his head. Yes, that was real enough. He'd fallen and bumped his head. And then what? Funny things did happen when you bumped your head. Perhaps you only saw Stigs when you fell and bumped your head.

He didn't think he wanted to fall over the cliff again on purpose and bump his head again.

Was Stig a person you could just go and play with like the children at the end of the road at home? He had to find out, but he didn't want to go to the chalk-pit and find – *nothing!* He stood with his hands in his pockets in the middle of the lawn, his fingers playing with something hard in the left-hand pocket of his jeans.

He remembered something, and pulled out the thing he had in his hand. Of course – the flint! He looked at it glinting in the sunlight, like a black diamond with its chipped pattern. He'd seen Stig make it! There was no mistake about that. Of course Stig was real!

He set off again at a run, climbed the fence into the paddock, and waded through the long wet grass the other side. The copse round the edge of the chalk-pit looked dark beyond the sunlit grass.

In the middle of the paddock he found himself slowing down and stopping again.

Something at the back of his mind was telling him that he'd seen pictures of chipped flints in books, and real ones in museums, and that they were made thousands of years ago by rough people who weren't alive any longer. People found them and put them in cases with notices on them. Perhaps he'd just found this one. And imagined everything else.

And supposing he hadn't imagined Stig, was he the sort of person who liked people coming to play?

Well, he told himself, all he really wanted to do was

to look at the place where he had fallen over yesterday. Have another look down the dump. There was that bicycle, anyway.

He walked to the edge of the paddock. A clump of brown grass jumped up from under his feet and bounced away towards a bramble patch, showing a white tail and two long ears. Barney's heart bumped, but it was only a rabbit. He ran after it, but it had disappeared in the thick of the undergrowth.

Feeling bolder, he climbed over the fence and went carefully towards the edge of the pit, making sure this time that he kept near a big tree that seemed to be well anchored to the side, and peeped over.

He could see the patch of raw earth and white chalk where the ground had given way under him, the dangling creepers lower down, and a scatter of broken chalk at the bottom. He craned over to see the hole he had made in the roof of the den. There was a pile of branches and rubbish against the foot of the cliff, but no gaping hole. Not a sign of a hole, of a roof, of a den – of a Stig. He listened. A blackbird turning over dry leaves in search of worms was making a noise much too big for itself. But apart from that the pit was silent and empty.

Barney walked away from the edge of the pit and climbed over the fence into the sunshine of the paddock, thinking hard. He looked at the stone in his hand, he felt the bump on his head. He had seen the raw patch where the ground had given way. He *remembered* crashing through a sort of roof and leaving a big gaping hole. And yet there wasn't a hole.

So he couldn't have made one.

But he must have landed somewhere. And he had that clear picture in his head of looking up through a hole at the side of the cliff and the clouds passing over the sky.

And suddenly, as he stood in the middle of the paddock, he gave a big jump as the answer came to him like getting a sum right.

If there wasn't a hole it was because somebody had *mended* it! Stig wasn't the sort of person to leave a large hole in his roof for long. Not his friend Stig!

All at once everything fitted together – yesterday's adventure on that Stiggish sort of afternoon, the bump on his head, the flint, and this bright Autumn morning when he was going to visit his friend Stig. And he was quite clear in his head now what he was going to do and how he was going to do it.

He set off running, back to the garden. Presents for Stig! When you visited people this time of year you always brought something from the garden: tomatoes you couldn't bottle or apples you hadn't room to store. He looked round the big old apple tree for windfalls. There were some big ones, difficult to manage without a basket, but he stuffed them into his shirt, making sure there weren't any wasps in them first. What else? He saw a line of carrots – his favourite fruit! He was allowed to pull up carrots, they were good for his teeth, so he heaved up a few good-sized ones and rubbed the earth off with his fingers. Then he had an idea and ran to the tool-shed where he found a ball of garden string. It was all right just to *borrow* it. Back he ran again, across the garden, over the fence, across the paddock, over into the copse, and through the brambles and dead leaves to the edge of the pit.

He sat himself comfortably on the trunk of the tree that curved out over the pit like the neck of a camel, and looked carefully again at what he could see. There was the broken edge of the cliff, there were the trailing creepers, there at the bottom were the scattered lumps of chalk that had come down with him. And now that he was really looking at it he could see a piece of new linoleum – well, not exactly new, nothing in the dump was new, but it looked as if it had been put there not long ago because it wasn't covered with moss like things that had been there for a long time. And he could see, at one side of this pile of branches and things that was Stig's lean-to roof, a faint path in the bottom of the pit that led to the front of the den.

He found the end of the ball of string and tied the bunch of carrots to it. Then he began to pay out the string, with the carrots dangling on the end, towards the bottom of the pit. He hoped it was long enough. There always seems to be miles of string in a ball, but it dwindled and dwindled as he lowered the carrots down, until he was afraid that it wouldn't reach the bottom. Bother! A cobble, a regular spider's-nest of tangled string appeared, and he had to stop to un-cobble it. At last, with a few feet in hand, the carrots were swinging on a level with Stig's front door. Barney's seat was not quite above it, so he had to get the carrots swinging to and fro, all that way beneath him, until they were actually knocking at the door like five pink fingers. Barney was bubbling so much with laughter inside him at the trick he was playing on Stig that he forgot to be dizzy.

'Stig!' he called down the pit. 'Morning, Stig! I'm knocking at your front door!' And suddenly, out from the stack of branches appeared the tousled head of Stig, and stayed there wagging to and fro, following the swinging carrots like a cat watching a pendulum. Barney nearly fell off the tree with laughing.

'Hallo Stig!' he called. 'Good morning! I'm Barney, you remember? How are you?'

Stig looked up, and for a moment Barney felt quite frightened at the ferocious scowl on his face, and was glad to be high up out of his reach. Should he have played a trick on Stig? Perhaps he didn't have what the grown-ups called a Sense of Humour. Did Stigs have sense of humours?

But when Stig made out who it was sitting above him his face suddenly changed, his big white teeth showed in a broad grin, he waved both his arms over his head, and he jumped about in the bottom of the pit to show how pleased he was.

'Have a carrot, Stig!' called Barney. 'For you,' he said, pointing to Stig. 'To eat,' he added. 'Good for your teeth!' he said, making biting movements. Stig leapt at the carrots as they swung past, caught them, looked at them closely, smelt them, then put one in his mouth and crunched it. He looked up at Barney, smiling with his mouth full, to show that he liked his present, then made signs which clearly meant that Barney was to come down.

'Well, I'm not going to jump this time,' said Barney. 'And this string's too thin to climb down. Going round!' he said, making circling movements with his arms. He got off his perch and walked the long way round the top of the pit to the shallow end where he had got out the night before.

It was more difficult finding his way to Stig's den along the floor of the pit than it had been finding his way out the night before. The dump looked quite different—more cheerful, with the sunlight pouring down through the golden autumn leaves, and the ash and sycamore seeds twiddling down from the trees on top. But the tail of the aeroplane was only part of a farm machine, and the ship's helm was a broken cartwheel.

There was the bicycle too, just a rusty frame with bits of brake hanging on to it. Never mind, he'd found something much more interesting, and he'd seen it and spoken to it in broad daylight. A real live Stig, and he was going to visit him.

That's if he could find his way among the giant nettles.

Suddenly, there was Stig, coming to meet him straight through a nettle patch as if stings meant nothing to him. Barney stopped. What now? Shake hands? Rub noses? — no, perhaps not! He remembered the apples he had stowed inside his shirt, took one out, and held it towards Stig on the palm of his hand as if he was trying to make friends with a horse.

'I hope you liked the carrots, Stig,' said Barney. 'Have an apple!' Stig took the apple quite politely between finger and thumb — not between his teeth, as Barney somehow expected him to — and sniffed it. Barney took out another apple for himself and bit into it.

'Good!' he said. 'Delicious!'

Stig took a bite, seemed to like it, smiled, and they both started walking towards the den, munching their apples. Stig just blundered through the nettles, and as far as Barney could see they *stung* him and raised bumps as they did on other people, but he just didn't care. Barney himself avoided the nettles as much as he could. He got stung once or twice but decided not to make a fuss about it. Stigs don't mind stings, he thought, so he'd better not.

Stig led the way to the den. Barney noticed several dumps of new white chalk near the path, and remembered the new tunnelling he had seen yesterday, and the baby's bath full of chalk.

'Been digging, Stig?' he asked, pointing to the dumps. Stig grinned and nodded.

It was gloomy and overhung at Stig's end of the pit even on this bright day, and the den itself, now that the hole in the roof was mended, was even darker. The teapot lamp was flickering and throwing a dim light on the den and the place where Stig had been digging, but it was not very cheerful.

Come to think of it, thought Barney, rabbits and things that live in holes don't have any light *at all*. Not much fun for them, with no windows. Couldn't he find some windows for Stig?

What made it worse was that Stig had started a small fire in the den part. He must have just done it, because Barney had not noticed any smoke when he was sitting on the tree-trunk. The smoke was filling the den, and there was no way out for it except to trickle through the gaps in the roof. It made Barney's eyes water, but he supposed it was one of the things you just had to put up with, like nettles. All the same, the place could do with a chimney, as well as windows.

He began to get used to the darkness, and he could see that the tunnel at the back of the cave went further back into the chalk than he had noticed. The digging tools were lying about: the bedstead leg, a broken cast-iron shoe-scraper, and an iron bar like the one he'd seen his father use on the jack to lift the car up.

Stig was reaching up to offer Barney another turnip, but Barney didn't feel like turnip so soon after breakfast.

'Can I help you dig, Stig?' he asked. 'I expect you're busy anyhow.' He went to the end of the tunnel and picked up the bit of bedstead, and began to attack the wall of chalk. It was not as easy as he had expected. The chalk in the inside of the hill here was firm, not crumbly as it was on the outside where the rain got at it. Barney's bashes with the awkward piece of metal only broke off smallish chips of chalk, and he was soon puffed.

Stig, who had been standing watching him, took the digger from his hands and showed him how to dig out a hollow at the bottom of the chalk wall, then knock down large chunks which came away easily because they were not held up underneath. There was soon a pile of loose chalk, and Barney picked it up with his hands and put it in the small tin bath. When it was full it was about as much as he could do to drag it along the floor of the cave towards the entrance. Stig helped him, and between them they lugged the load out of the den and dumped it. But Barney noticed that Stig took care to put it some way from his door. He supposed that piles of new white chalk would let people know that something was going on.

Stig let him dig next time, and he soon got the hang of cutting under and letting it tumble down from the top. Now and then they would come to a great flint embedded in the chalk, like a fossil monster with knobs and bulges, and they would have to chip round it, worry it, and loosen it like a tooth until at last it came free, usually bringing down a lot of chalk with it. They worked on happily for quite a time, taking it in turns to dig and load, and now and then they would stop for a break and take a drink of water from the tin or eat a refreshing apple.

Barney's jeans were white with chalk dust, and his hair and nails were full of it. He suddenly wondered what his Grandmother would say – then he suddenly wondered what time it was! In spite of the apples his tummy was telling him that it might be lunch time.

'You haven't got a clothes-brush, have you Stig?' he asked. Stig looked blank and Barney decided that he probably hadn't. His eye fell on Stig's water-pipe. Somebody had thrown away a vacuum-cleaner, so there must be one of the brush things somewhere. Sure enough he spied one, fixed as a sort of T-piece on the end of a long thin pole that was helping to hold the roof up. He thought the roof might hold itself up for a bit while he got the worst of the chalk dust off with the vacuum-cleaner end, and it did. Stig was watching with a puzzled look, wondering why Barney should be pulling down part of his roof to brush at his clothes with.

'You're lucky, Stig,' said Barney. 'Nobody asks you how you got in such a mess. I've got to go now. Must be nearly lunch-time. Pity I can't ask you to lunch, but . . .' But really, he thought, nobody else even *believes* in him yet.

'I'll be back this afternoon,' Barney said from the door. 'Thanks for letting me help you. Good-bye!'

Grandmother and Lou were late getting back from the town, so he had time to get the chalk out of his nails and hair and to look fairly respectable for lunch. They were too full of talk about how they had spent their morning to question him much about what *he* had been doing.

Over the stewed apples he was able to say quietly: 'Granny, have you got any things you don't want?'

'Things I don't want, dear?' Grandmother repeated. 'What sort of things? Chilblains? Grandchildren?'

'No, Granny. I mean – things like windows and chimneys.'

Grandmother thought about this for a moment, and then said that really she couldn't think of anything *like* windows and chimneys except windows and chimneys, and she thought the house had only just enough of these to go round. And Lou just laughed and said, '*Really*, Barney!'

Then Grandmother said that it did remind her there were some tins and jam-jars she had meant to put out for the dustbin man, and perhaps Barney would be a dear and carry them to the gate.

*

There were more jam-jars than Barney had thought possible, and quite a lot of useful tins, the sort with lids. Barney looked at them. The dustbin man wouldn't say thank you for them, he thought. Why shouldn't Stig have them?

He remembered a big wooden box which Grandfather had helped him fix wheels on to, so that he and Lou could use it as a cart. He searched round and found it among the firewood, but still with its four wheels more or less straight and the piece of rope on the front to pull it with. He loaded it with jam-jars and tins, and found it quite a weight when he set off across the paddock with it. He looked at Flash, the pony, as he struggled through a clump of long grass and called rather crossly: 'You might come and help pull, instead of standing there!' But he knew that Flash took a lot of persuading to be caught for Lou to ride him, let alone for pulling carts. The pony just stood and watched, tossing his head now and then at the afternoon flies.

By the time Barney had got his load to the edge of the pit he was quite tired, but there was still the problem of getting them to the bottom. He sat on the camel's-neck tree-trunk. The string was still there. It was the thick brown sort, and he thought it would be strong enough for a few jam-jars.

He called to Stig, and after a time Stig came out backwards, like a badger with its bedding, dragging a load of chalk.

'I've got some things for you, Stig!' Barney called. He pulled up the string and took the end to the pile of jam-jars. About eight of them were packed in a cardboard box. It would take too long to pass them down one by one, so he tied the string round the box, took it carefully along the tree-trunk, and started to lower it. This wasn't nearly as easy as the carrots. The box swung wildly, the string round it started slipping, the part he was holding tried to run through his fingers and burned his hands. He took a turn round the stump of a branch and let it run out round that, hardly daring to look down and see what was happening. He hoped Stig wouldn't get a jam-jar on his head.

The box was hanging by one corner when it reached

the ground, but instead of untying it Stig disappeared into his den.

'Hey! Stig! Undo it!' Barney called. 'There's some more to come.'

Stig came out again holding what was left of a large broad-brimmed lady's straw hat, with ribbons to tie it under the chin. He untied the string from the box and tied it to the ribbons. It made quite a useful-looking cargo-sling.

'Jolly good idea, Stig!' Barney shouted. Stig's got brains, he thought.

After that it was quite easy. He hauled up the hat, filled it with jam-jars, lowered it down with the string running round the stump of branch, waited for Stig to unload, hauled it up again, and so on. When he had finished the jam-jars he started on the tins, which were much lighter. And when he had lowered all the tins he looked at the truck.

How strong is string? he wondered. Could he send the truck down the same way? If he didn't he would have to trundle it all the way round the top and along the bottom of the pit.

He wound the string a few times round the branch-stump, leaving enough loose to reach the truck on the cliff-top, humped himself along the tree-trunk, tied the string to a wheel of the truck, moved back along the trunk, and pulled the truck towards him by the string. The truck lurched over the edge of the cliff, swung wildly outwards on the string, which ran out so fast that he couldn't stop it – until a tangle in the string made it stop with a jerk, the string broke, and the truck was falling through the air.

Barney held on for dear life to the tree, with his face against the mossy bark, and shut his eyes. He felt weak and dizzy.

At last he allowed himself to look down. He couldn't see the truck at first. Then he saw that it had swung out to land in the branches of an elder tree, and was hanging there quite happily.

'I've sent the truck down,' he called to Stig. 'It may come in useful.'

He was still feeling what his Grandmother used to call hot-and-cold-all-over, but he carefully inched himself off the tree and on to firm ground, and set off round and down to the pit. A pity he couldn't let himself down on a rope – but no, he thought, he wouldn't try just yet.

His idea of sending the things down on the string had been a good one though, he thought to himself as he walked through the copse. Another day he'd have to find some more tins and jam-jars to send down. He hoped Stig liked them. They would come in useful for – for – well, things like that always came in useful. If you kept them long enough.

By the time he got to the den, Stig had untangled the truck from the tree, and was squatting looking at it, and at the tins and jam-jars. And then Barney wondered what they *were* going to do with them.

'These are jam-jars, Stig', he explained. 'Jam and marmalade come in them, and you can use them for keeping stuff in them – rice and coffee and things like that.' But did Stig *want* to keep rice and coffee in his den? 'And these are tins. They're empty of course, but you get all sorts of things in tins. Peaches and baked

beans. You have to open them with an opener like
this.'

He took out of his pocket a tin-opener which he
usually carried about with him. It was the sort with a
butterfly handle which you had to turn. Just to show,
he fitted it on to the bottom of one of the empty tins
and twisted the handle. The opener crept round the
edge of the tin, the blade ploughed into the metal at
the bottom, and soon the shiny round disc of metal
came loose.

Stig was fascinated. He looked at the flat round piece
of tin which had been the bottom, he looked at the
empty tube which was all that was left of the rest of it.
And he took the tin-opener from Barney and turned
the handle, but he couldn't make it out.

'It's quite easy, Stig. Look!' and Barney took
another tin, fitted the opener on the bottom, and
showed him how to work it. And there was another
round plate and another tin tube. Then Stig had to
have a go, and they started on a third.

One of the tins had been rather flattened, but it gave
Barney an idea for how it might be used. He took it,
left Stig with the others, and towed the truck into the
den and along to the place where Stig had been digging
at the chalk. There was quite a lot of loose rubble
lying about there, and Barney set to work to shovel it
into the truck with the flattened tin. It was certainly
better than using his hands, though it wasn't quite the
right sort of shovel-shape yet. He hammered at it with
an unbroken flint-stone and made it into quite a handy
scoop, like the sort the village grocer used for shovel-
ling sugar into little paper bags.

He toiled away until the truck was heaped full. It held much more chalk than the tin bath, and because of its wheels he could pull it away quite easily.

'Look, Stig!' he said as he went past where Stig was sitting. 'Look at all the chalk I've loaded.' But Stig seemed too busy to notice.

Barney wheeled the truck along to the place where they were now dumping the chalk, and tipped out his load. Then he ran back to the den, with the truck bouncing along empty behind him. When he got back, Stig was sitting there surrounded by round plates of tin and empty tubes, and just in the act of taking the bottom out of the last tin.

'Stig, what are you doing?' exclaimed Barney. 'You've spoiled all the tins now! You can't keep things in tins with no bottoms!' He was really quite annoyed. What *was* the use of a lot of tin tubes with no ends?

Stig sat there playing with them. He seemed to have the idea of fitting one inside the other, but that wouldn't work because they were all exactly the same size. However, one of them that had got a bit pinched did fit into another, which seemed to please him a lot.

Barney thought it was a bit childish of Stig to sit there playing, like a baby with plastic bricks, when there was all that work to be done. But Stig went on seriously worrying over the problem of fitting them together. He found that by pinching together the end of a tin he could *make* it fit into the next one, and soon he had four or five fitted together like a length of stove-pipe.

Stove-pipe! Barney *knew* there was something Stig needed badly.

'You *are* clever, Stig!' he said. 'You've made a chimney!'

Stig looked blank. He didn't know he needed a chimney. He didn't know what a chimney was. Certainly he'd made one, but if it hadn't been for Barney he wouldn't have known.

Working together, they fitted all the tins one into the other until they had a pipe that was taller than

either of them. With Barney directing, they carried it into the smoky den, where it was too long to stand upright.

'Now all we've got to do is poke it through the roof,' said Barney. Stig looked doubtfully at him, but together they managed quite easily to push it through a crack between the piece of linoleum and a sheet of corrugated iron. But now what? They couldn't just leave it hanging above the fire.

'I know!' exclaimed Barney. 'The bath!' He left

Stig patiently holding the chimney, and went and fetched the tin bath. What luck! It had a rusty hole in the bottom which only needed a little work with the boot-scraper to make it big enough to fit the chimney through. Stig was dimly beginning to see what Barney was trying to do. Together they built up a fireplace of chalk-blocks and big flints, rested the bath upside-down on top – and there was mantelpiece and chimney, with the flue leading from the hole in the up-turned bath, through the roof, and into the open air.

Barney lit the fire – which Stig had laid as they built the fireplace – and threw some additional scraps of paper and twigs on to it. Once the smoke had learnt its way it went roaring up the pipe. They rushed outside and there it was coming out of what looked like a proper chimney-pot sticking through the roof. Stig watched, fascinated.

'There you are, Stig,' said Barney. 'Now you've got a proper fireplace people can come and visit you without getting their eyes full of smoke.' Actually Stig didn't seem to care very much about having the place full of smoke, but he was as pleased with his fireplace as if it had been a new toy, and kept on putting twigs and leaves on the fire so that he could go out and see the smoke coming out the other end. And Barney was so proud of his invention that he looked round for something else to invent.

He saw the stack of jam-jars. What had he brought those for? It would be too dull just to use them to keep food in. Stig's den wasn't that sort of place. He had to think of a new way of using jam-jars.

What had he thought Stig's house needed most? A

chimney – he'd got that now. A chimney and – yes, a window! A *window*.

Well, windows were made of glass, and so were jam-jars. Yes, but the *shape*! Doors were made of wood and so were clothes-pegs; ships were made of steel and so were tin-openers. But you can't make a ship out of tin-openers or a door out of clothes-pegs. The shape's wrong.

You couldn't hammer glass flat, could you? He picked up the boot scraper. No, of course not.

Stig had stacked the jars on top of each other, lying on their sides. They made a sort of wall of glass like that. But they rolled about, and of course there were gaps between the jars.

Barney looked at one side of the den, the darkest side, which really needed windows. It was built of wooden boxes from the dump, bottoms outward, open tops inward. He took the digging-tool and knocked the bottom out of one. There was now an open square where the daylight came in. But so did the wind, and Stig didn't seem at all pleased at sitting in a draught.

Stigs like to be snug, thought Barney.

He carried the jars in and stacked them in the frame of the box. They fitted quite well, the light came in, but the draught came in too.

Stig got up and looked at the gaps between the jars, grunted, and went out of the den. Barney followed him, wondering. Stig led the way along the bottom of the cliff to where there had lately been a landslide and quite a large chunk of cliff-top had come down in one piece. Between the topsoil and the chalk there was a layer of red clay, good damp squidgy stuff you could make model animals with. Stig began to dig out lumps of clay with his fingers, and Barney found another good clay-mine and did the same. They got as much as they could carry and took it back to the den, and from the outside Stig set to work to fill in the gaps between the jam-jars. They had to make two more journeys before all the jars were firmly bedded in clay, and then Barney carefully wiped the smears off the bottoms of the jars with a rag.

Then they stood and admired their window. They even made faces at each other, one standing inside and the other outside, because you could almost *see* through it. It certainly let the light in, even though it was late in the afternoon and there was not much light to *let* in.

'Well, well,' said Barney. 'That's that!' It was a thing he had often heard his Grandfather say when he'd finished a job.

He was tired after all the inventing he had done. He went to sit down, and then he saw all the round plates of tin that Stig had cut out, lying around on the floor. He gathered them up. There must be a use for these, too. He went back to the window, and found that the discs fitted exactly over the ends of the jars if he pressed them into the soft clay. There were just enough to go round.

'There you are, Stig,' he said. 'Like on a ship, to shut the port-holes. If you don't want people to look in. Or to shut the dark out.'

There was a feeling in the evening air that darkness was coming and that it would be snug to sit by the new fireplace and watch the fire going up the chimney. But

Barney suddenly remembered something and stood up with his mouth open.

'Stig,' he said. 'I've got to go home. All the way home I mean. I probably won't be staying with Granny till Christmas.'

Stig looked at him.

'Stig,' said Barney. 'When I come back again, you — you will still be here, won't you?'

Stig didn't answer, but he went to a little niche in the chalk wall, poked about among some things there and brought back something which he gave to Barney. He looked at it. It was a little chipped flint, perfectly shaped like a flat Christmas-tree, and very sharp.

'An arrow-head?' Barney gasped. 'For me? Oh, *thank you* Stig! I — I really must go now. See you at Christmas. You will be here at Christmas, won't you, Stig? Good bye!' And he ran off.

As he made his way along the bottom of the pit he felt he knew the way there better than anywhere else in the world. And he felt that Stig's house was as much his home as anywhere else. After all, it was like drawing pictures. Once you've put a chimney and a window on a house, you've really *made* a house.

3. It Warms You Twice

CHRISTMAS was over at Grandmother's house. The old oak beams were still decorated with trails of ivy and there were still branches of holly stuck in the tops of picture-frames. The last turkey-bone had been picked, the last thimble found in the pudding. They had even got a good way round the Christmas cake. They had been to a circus.

Barney lay in bed in the grey morning light. For once he was not in a hurry to jump out of bed. The air in the bedroom felt icy to the end of his nose. 'Let me see,' he thought, 'is there anything special to look forward to today?' He couldn't think of anything.

He was looking at the thick black beam in the wall

that grew out of the floor right up to the ceiling. It had been part of a ship before it was part of the house, Grandfather said. It had deep holes cut out of it where other bits of timber had fitted into it. What was that hidden in one of the holes?

Barney sat up in bed suddenly. It was the flint! Stig's flint, left there since last time he had come to stay. And he hadn't even *thought* about Stig all over Christmas.

He got out of bed and looked out of the window. There was white frost on the grass. A few hopeful birds hung about the bird table, fluffed up like woolly balls, waiting for some food to be put out for them. He reached up and took out the flint. It was like a lump of ice.

'I wonder what it's like living in a cave these days,' thought Barney. 'Poor Stig! He must be cold.'

After breakfast Barney slipped out of the house and went off to the pit. In the copse the frozen leaves crunched like cornflakes under his feet. He climbed down into the pit on the far side, where the cliff was lowest, and it hurt his fingers to hold on to the icy tree roots. The nettles were all dead in the bottom of the pit and the old cans had lumps of solid ice in them.

There was no sign of life in the shelter, though he noticed the ashes of a small dead fire and a faint smell of wood-smoke still hung around. But at the back of the cave was a kind of nest made of bracken and dead grass and newspaper. He thought he heard breathing sounds coming out of it.

'Stig!' Barney called. Nothing happened. I wonder

if he's like a dormouse, he thought, and goes to sleep all the winter.

He called again. 'Stig! Are you there?'

There was a rustle in the nest, and a mop of black hair poked up out of it. Underneath it was Stig's face, but it was screwed up in a very strange expression.

'Is he cross?' wondered Barney anxiously.

His eyes still screwed up and his mouth shut, Stig took a deep breath.

Then he sneezed. It was a sneeze like a cannon going off, and it made the cave echo.

'You did give me a fright!' said Barney. 'You've got a cold, Stig. No wonder, when you live in this damp place. You need a good fire.'

He looked around the shelter and the cave. There didn't seem to be any wood to burn. Stig's heavy flint axe was leaning against the wall and Barney picked it up, but he saw that the edge was crumbled and blunt.

'You'll have to sharpen this,' said Barney.

Stig crawled out of his nest, blinking stupidly. He moved as if his joints were rusty and he did not take the axe as Barney held it out to him.

'All right, I'll do it then,' said Barney. 'I expect it's quite easy.' He sat down with the axe between his knees and picked up a heavy iron bolt and tried to remember how he had seen Stig chip the flint. But it was painful holding the cold flint and the cold iron and his fingers were so clumsy that they would not do what he wanted them to.

'Oh, never mind,' said Barney. 'Come on, we've *got* to get some wood.' He stood up with the axe and went out of the shelter. Stig followed, half awake, half frozen, and silent. They climbed up out of the pit and looked around the copse for wood to cut. Barney could see now that someone, probably Stig, had already been chopping and breaking down the dry branches. He chose a fairly thin thorn tree and set to work on it.

The axe swung, the tree shook, the flint bounced off the tough bark, but he didn't seem to be getting anywhere. Stig just squatted miserably on a bank, with his arms wrapped round his knees.

'Here, you have a go!' puffed Barney. 'It'll warm you up anyhow. My Grandfather always says wood warms you twice, once when you cut it and once when you burn it.'

He handed the axe to Stig, but Stig only looked at it sadly and shook his head. Barney got worried. He really must do something about Stig. Suddenly he had an idea.

'Wait here, Stig!' he said. 'I won't be long.'

Barney ran off through the copse and up the field towards the house. He went to the shed at the back and got his Grandfather's big steel axe and the long sharp cross-cut saw – and what else did he need? Yes, a coil of rope. He slung it over his shoulder and made off again down the field to the copse.

'Here you are, Stig!' he called, as he came up to Stig still huddled on the bank.

The sight of the shining steel axe worked like medicine on Stig. He uncurled himself and picked up the axe by its long handle. He tried its sharp edge with his thumb. He weighed it in his hands and swung it like a golfer testing a new club. His black eyes lit up and he looked around for something to use his new weapon on.

Standing among the saplings of the copse was a tall ash tree with a trunk at least two feet thick. Stig marched up to it, swinging the axe.

'Oh, no!' cried Barney. 'You mustn't! Not that one, Stig!'

But there was no stopping Stig. At the first blow the blade bit deep into the tree. White chips flew as he swung again and again.

Barney hopped round him excitedly. 'Stig,' he called. 'Do you think you ought to? Oh Stig, isn't it too *big*, Stig? *Stig*, I didn't know you were such a chopper! Well done Stig! Stig, Stig, let me have a go!'

There was soon a great wedge cut into the side of the tree, but it was still only half-way through. Stig stopped for a rest and they both looked at the tree. It swayed a little in the light breeze.

'You know what, Stig?' said Barney. 'It's going to fall and smash the fence if we're not careful. I better tie a rope to it.'

He slung the coil of rope round him and pulled himself up by the lower branches of the tree. He had climbed most of the trees round about before, but he had never climbed one that was already chopped half-way through. He supposed he should have tied the rope on before they had started cutting. As he climbed higher he could feel something different about the swaying of this tree. It did not have the springy exciting sway of a sound tree. It was only swaying a few inches but at the end of each sway you had the feeling that it was waiting, not quite sure whether it would sway back again or whether it would just go on and fall. He tied

44

the rope to the trunk as high up as he dared, threw the rope outwards and watched it uncoil to the ground, and scrambled down again himself.

'Now we ought to saw it on the other side,' said Barney. 'I've seen Grandfather do it.' He picked up the big cross-cut saw. 'Here, you take the other end,' he told Stig.

Stig looked at the saw doubtfully. He felt its sharp teeth and grunted approval, but he still did not understand what they were going to do with it.

'Look,' said Barney. 'You hold that end and I hold this end. I pull and then you pull. It's easy once you get started.'

Stig still looked a bit blank. They scraped away clumsily at the bark of the tree-trunk until at last the saw teeth cut a straight groove and settled into it. Stig's eyes widened as the sawdust began to fly and he pumped the handle furiously.

'Ouch!' cried Barney. 'You're pulling too far. You've made me skin my knuckles.'

'Steady!' cried Barney. 'Must we go so fast? We've got a long way to go yet.'

'Stop!' cried Barney. 'Look, Stig, you're pushing as well as pulling. It makes the saw bend and it makes you tired too.'

At last they settled down to a steady in – out, snore-snore. The blade sang as it bit deeper into the wood and the sawdust spurted out each end. Then the whole thing seemed to get sticky, and at last, however hard they struggled, they could not move it either way.

'Bother!' said Barney. 'Now what?'

They stood back and looked at the tree. The weight of branches on one side was making the trunk lean that way and closing up the crack the saw had made.

'We'll have to pull,' said Barney.

Stig and he took the end of the rope and heaved. The crest of the tree came slowly towards them, hung still, and swayed back again. They heaved again. This

time the tree seemed to come a little further, hung longer, but still it swung back. With their third pull, as it rocked towards them there came a cracking sound from the trunk.

'It's coming!' cried Barney excitedly.

The tree swayed away from them again, but they heaved again and this time there were more splintering cracks.

'Once more!' shouted Barney.

They tugged, the tree rocked slowly, hung at the end of its swing, then instead of rocking back again lurched further over towards them. From the trunk came a splitting, rending, screeching sound, and Stig and Barney turned and ran. Barney heard an appalling rush and crash and splintering of branches behind him as the crest hit the ground, and the topmost twigs thrashed the back of his legs as he ran.

They turned round to look. Barney's heart was bouncing with excitement.

'Phew, we've done it!' he gasped, gaping at the ruin they had made and the great empty hole they had left in the sky line. 'What a lot of firewood!'

*

That afternoon Barney brought a hatchet, iron wedges, and the big sledge-hammer down to the copse. Stig and he trimmed off the smaller branches, cut up the boughs into long logs, and managed, after long and patient sawing, to cut the main trunk into three. Then they set to work to split it up. This seemed to be a thing Stig understood. They started a split with the axe, put in an iron wedge, drove it in with the hammer to make the split grow, then drove in other wedges until at last there was a satisfying SCHPLITTTT! – and the fibres of the timber parted from end to end.

The sky was now getting grey and dark and an icy wind had begun to blow, but they did not notice it. It warms you twice, cutting wood! They trundled the logs to the edge of the pit, and sent them crashing to the bottom – not too near the den. Barney looked up at the pale sunset and saw a kind of dust floating down from the sky. Sawdust? No, as it settled on the ground it was white. It was fine snow.

'Come on, Stig, let's get the fire going!' said Barney. They went round to the entrance to the pit and along the bottom to the shelter, humped what they thought were enough logs and kindling inside, and then sat down, very tired, on the floor of the dark den. 'Now for a nice fire,' thought Barney.

Stig stirred himself. He picked up the gear-lever of a motor-car that was lying around the den and poked carefully at the ashes of what had been the fire. But they were well and truly dead. Stig sighed. Then he reached for his bow, which was propped against the wall. It was a fine steel bow, made out of a springy television aerial and strung with picture wire. He took the leg of a hardwood chair, which was sharpened to a point at one end. He fitted the point into a hole in a block of wood which he held with his toes, passed the bowstring round the leg of the chair, held the top of the chair leg with a cracked egg-cup, and began to draw the bow backwards and forwards so that the string made the chair leg twirl. Barney watched fascinated as Stig worked away, but though Stig seemed warm enough at the job, Barney was getting cold. At last the point of the chair leg twirling in the block of wood began to smoke. Stig quickly fed it with a handful of grass and started blowing on it, still fiddling away frantically with the bow. The grass glowed, Stig fiddled and blew, but everything in the cave was damp and the little fire died out with a wisp of smoke. The bowstring frayed and snapped. Stig, exhausted, said something in his strange language, threw the chair leg across the cave and sat there biting his nails.

'D'you want a *light*, Stig?' asked Barney brightly, and he took a box of matches from his pocket and struck one. The little flame suddenly lit up the cave.

The effect on Stig was amazing. He uncurled himself and leapt to his feet in a bound, and stood staring at the lighted match with round eyes. When the flame burnt down to Barney's fingers and he had to blow it out, Stig gave a sort of despairing moan.

'It's all right, Stig. I've got lots more,' Barney said. He struck another and Stig jumped again, but this time crept up to stare at it close to.

'Come on, let's have some paper and twigs,' said Barney. By the light of a third match they found some, but they were not very dry and it took another three or four to get a little fire going. Stig was lying on his stomach blowing like a bellows, now gently, now fiercely, adding a twig here and a splinter from a wooden box there, building a careful pile, feeding the fire where it was needed. At last the flames licked upwards, the smoke began to clear itself through the hole in the bath and a warm glow began to light up the walls of the cave. Stig put two big logs crossed at the back of the fire, and they began hissing and sizzling happily.

Stig stretched himself out in the warmth like a cat, then held out his hand to Barney as if asking for something. Barney handed him the matchbox.

'You want me to show you how to strike a match, Stig? Here, push the little drawer thing! That's right, but not too far. Take out a match. Now you better shut the box. Hold the match by the white end, not the black end, silly! Now rub it on the side of the box. No, the *side*. There!'

After one or two tries Stig managed to strike the match. He held the little flame and gazed at it until he burnt his fingers and he had to drop it.

'Go on, strike another!' urged Barney. 'Granny's got plenty. A box only costs about a penny, I think.'

But Stig wouldn't waste another. He took the box and hid it in his bed. It was clear he thought a match was a very precious thing indeed.

Stig came back to the fire with his hands full of chestnuts. He put them in the ashes and they lay and waited until the chestnuts popped, then they hooked them out with the gear-lever and blew on them and ate them. There were plenty of nuts in Stig's hoard, and Barney ate twenty-three. He felt wonderfully full and warm, and he lay looking at the fire and at the shadows dancing on the walls of the cave.

But Stig was squatting with a far-away look in his eyes and a piece of charred board in his hand, looking towards a blank wall of the cave. He seemed to be looking through it, not at it. He moved up to the wall, his eyes fixed intently as though he was watching something interesting through a window. Then suddenly he attacked the white wall with his blackened stick. On the chalk he made sweeping black lines – and there was the outline of a galloping horse! More fierce scrapes of the stick – and there was a stag with antlers, galloping. Soon there were little men running with spears and bows and arrows.

Barney was hopping with excitement. 'Stig, you *are* a good drawer! I wish I could do pictures like that. Do some more, Stig! Oooh! The men are killing the deer!' For there was a spear, stuck in the shoulder of a galloping deer, so that it hurt to look at it.

But Stig took no notice and did not seem to be aware of Barney. For Stig was not thinking about making pictures. He was out there with the hunt, galloping with the animals, running with the hunters. And his hands, practised as they were at working with hard flint and tough bone, went on drawing the springy black lines on the white wall as if they could not help it.

Barney watched the hunting scene grow on the cave wall, and the last thing he thought about was the time. There was no clock in Stig's cave – not one that went anyway. He went back to the fire to make it up and caught a glimpse of the darkness outside the entrance. It was night! And he had to go back to the house through the dark, alone.

'Stig, I've got to go,' he said, but Stig didn't hear. Barney looked at Stig's collection of weapons leaning up against the entrance. There was a spear, with a long shaft of smooth hazelwood and a head of gleaming flint. It quivered when he picked it up as if it were alive.

'Stig, can I borrow one of your spears to see me home?' Barney asked. Stig turned his head, saw Barney with the spear, and grinned. Barney took that as permission to have the spear, though Stig was still probably lost in the excitement of the hunt. Barney took a piece of wood from the fire, one end of which was flaming brightly, and with the spear in the other hand he crept out. It was pitch dark and very cold. An icy wind made the flame of his torch flicker. He hoped it wouldn't go out. As he made his way along the bottom of the pit he kept his spear ready, just in case. Perhaps the bears and things were asleep for the winter. Perhaps there weren't any bears. After all, this was Nowadays, wasn't it? The only dangerous things were motor-cars when you crossed the road. Or *was* it Nowadays? It was difficult to feel sure in the dark at the bottom of the pit.

There was something squatting in his path. Barney gripped his spear tightly and held it poised. It was all right, it was a big can, with 'SLAPITON PAINT' printed on it. He gave it a friendly kick as he passed it. He climbed up into the copse and as he went through the trees a white thing swept towards him through the air. Without thinking he jabbed at it wildly with his spear, but the owl – for that's what it was – swerved away sharply and ghosted off into the dark. 'Off with you, Mr Owl,' said Barney crossly. 'What do you mean by trying to frighten me?'

He was soon out of the copse, and by the time he reached the house he was sorry to have to come in out of the dark. He put out the torch in the water-butt, put the spear in the broom cupboard, and changed his shoes.

His grandmother and sister were sitting at the table eating crumpets.

'Barney, where *have* you been? Were you up in your room all this time?'

'No, Granny. I'm sorry I'm late, but I've been out with Stig.'

'You've been out in the cold and dark all this time! Oh *Barney*!'

'I wasn't cold, really Granny. But poor Stig was nearly frozen to death and I had to warm him up and his axe wasn't sharp enough to cut down the little trees so we cut down a big one and the saw got stuck so I had to climb up it and pull it down and then we cut it up and pushed it down the pit. And Stig tried to light the fire with a chair leg and an egg-cup and a television aerial but I showed him how to strike matches and we ate chestnuts. And Lou, Stig's jolly good at drawing horses and things and he was still drawing them when I left with a piece of black board on the chalk.'

Lou giggled. 'Granny, Barney said Stig was drawing with a blackboard on the chalk. He meant a chalk on the blackboard.'

Barney decided to join in the laughter. They didn't ask him any more questions after that. But Barney felt happier about helping Stig with his firewood than he did about all the presents he had got for Christmas.

4. Gone A-Hunting

Lou had gone hunting. The North Kent Fox-hounds were meeting near Grandmother's house that day and a neighbour had offered to take Lou along and look after her. Grandmother had not been sure, but Lou had insisted that there was the pony, and she knew how to ride, so why shouldn't she? When the morning came it was pouring with rain, as it had been for days, but Lou said that hunting people didn't take any notice of the weather. So she had gone clattering off on the pony with the other riders, splashing through the puddles in the lane. Barney thought she looked a bit smug, but maybe it was just the rain trickling down her neck that made her turn her nose up.

Barney stood by the window looking at the weeping grey clouds.

'I'll take you in the car if you like, Barney,' said his grandmother. 'We could follow along the lanes.'

'No,' said Barney. 'Thank you,' he added.

'You'd rather just amuse yourself, dear?'

Barney nodded. He wandered off through the gloomy house, feeling sorry for himself. A cat saw him coming and must have seen the expression on his face, for it turned and bolted through the hall and into the back kitchen, where it shot into the broom cupboard. Barney went after it, but when he got to the broom cupboard he remembered something,

Yes, there among the brooms and mops and feather dusters was Stig's spear. He untangled it from all the other handles and brought it out into the light. He gave it a rub with a duster and the flint blade glinted. He shook it and the smooth wooden shaft quivered. It was a real hunting spear, there was no doubt about that. And Barney's face suddenly lightened.

Lou wasn't the only one who could go hunting!

Barney looked out at the wintry sky. Hunting people didn't take any notice of the weather, he thought. All the same, since nobody had told him he ought to, he decided to put on his rubber boots and mackintosh and sou'wester hat. He felt like a whaler with a harpoon.

He squelched through the empty paddock and into the dripping copse. He was glad to see that there was a wisp of smoke coming from Stig's end of the pit, and a smell of wood smoke hung about the copse. He went round to the entrance of the pit. At the bottom was a lake of rainwater with old cans and light-bulbs floating sadly around in it. But Stig was there in his den, sitting quite contentedly by a cheerful fire. He looked alarmed at first, not recognizing Barney in all his rainwear, but as soon as he saw Barney's face under the sou'wester he grinned.

'Hullo Stig!' called Barney. 'Would you like to come hunting with me?'

Stig went on grinning, but made no move.

'Hunting, Stig!' urged Barney. 'Foxes! Seek 'em out, Stig!' Barney made fierce stabbing motions with the spear, and galloping movements in his rubber boots, and even imitated a hunting horn: 'Tara, tara, taraaa!' Stig started to look excited, but he was still puzzled.

Barney took his hat off and scratched his head. How was he to explain to Stig about the meet of the foxhounds, and how he wanted them to join in? He looked at the drawings on the wall of the cave and they gave him an idea. He put down the spear and picked up a charred stick.

'Look, Stig,' he said. 'Fox!' And he carefully did his best drawing of a fox on the wall of the cave.

Stig looked alarmed, if anything, but Barney went on drawing. 'Hounds, Stig!' he said. Stig's eyes grew very big and round, but his face did not yet show that he understood what it was all about. Crackers! thought Barney, I'll have to draw the horses now. But Stig had already drawn some horses, so he only had to copy. He was rather pleased with his horse and at last Stig seemed to understand. I'll have to put someone riding the horse, thought Barney. I'll do Lou. There's the reins and there's her riding stick.

There was something about this human figure actually on top of the animal that really seemed to excite Stig. His eyes blazed, and he jumped up and seized his best bow and a handful of arrows, and looked hopefully at Barney like a dog that knows it's going to be taken on an exciting walk.

'Good old Stig!' cried Barney. 'That's the idea. Come on, let's go!' And without even thinking of putting on any extra clothes against the wintry weather, Stig danced out into the rain and Barney with him.

From deep in the distant woods came the toot of a hunting horn. Barney and Stig set out off across country towards it, down the muddy cart track that tunnelled into the woods, and into the fir plantation. As they trod softly over the carpet of fallen fir-needles Stig suddenly stiffened and raised his bow. Barney looked up. At the top of a fir tree was a squirrel, stripping a fir-cone.

Barney pulled Stig's arm. 'Don't fool about, Stig!' he said. 'It's foxes we're supposed to be hunting, not squirrels. Come on or we'll never find the hunt!'

The squirrel shook its tail, ran to the end of the branch, and sprang into the next tree, where it disappeared. Stig looked a bit annoyed, but he lowered his bow and they went on their way. They came into a woodland of tall sweet-chestnut trees and oaks. As they came near one of the oak trees Stig dropped to the ground and began crawling carefully forward.

'What is it, Stig?' asked Barney in a loud whisper. 'Is it a fox? Where, Stig? I can't see anything.'

Without looking round Stig waved his hand as if he wanted Barney to get down too. He dropped to his hands and knees, on to a bramble.

'Ouch!' yelped Barney. 'It's prickly!' And as he did so, a flock of six, twelve, no it must have been more than twenty wood-pigeons sprang into the air and flew off with a great beating of wings, every one of them stuffed with fallen acorns which they had been gorging. Stig let loose an arrow into the flying flock, but somehow failed to hit anything.

'Oh, *sorry*, Stig!' said Barney. 'I didn't know it was pigeons. Still we're not *supposed* to be hunting pigeons, you know. People don't. When they go fox-hunting they don't take any notice of anything else.'

But this time there was such a fierce scowl on Stig's face that Barney began to feel almost afraid of him. They walked in silence down a woodland track which held great pools of rainwater. Stig splashed through them without seeming to care how muddy his legs were getting. Barney waded more slowly behind, rather worried that the water might come over the tops of his boots. He saw Stig fit another arrow and raise his bow again. Across the track ahead strutted a proud cock pheasant, and before it knew what was happening Stig's flint-tipped arrow struck. With a pounce, Stig picked up the body of the pheasant, pulled the arrow out, and stuck the pheasant behind him into his girdle. The long brown feathers wagged as if he had sprouted a tail as he walked on, but Barney was not at all happy about killing this pheasant. It was bound to be poaching, or the wrong time of year, or not sporting to shoot them except with a real gun and cartridges, or something. It would have been better to stick to squirrels and wood-pigeons. But he did not say anything this time.

The tootling of the horn was getting nearer now and there were crashings in thickets and the voice of the huntsman encouraging the hounds. Stig stopped and looked about him, and Barney ran and caught up with him.

'It's the hunt, Stig,' he said. 'There must be foxes here somewhere. Keep a good look out and we might see one.'

The crashings and voices seemed quite close, and Barney suddenly thought that perhaps the huntsmen would be angry if they found them in the middle of the wood, especially with a poached pheasant. There was a bank with a sort of little cave under the exposed roots of a beech tree, and Barney pulled Stig into this. As they lay hidden there they both sniffed. There was a strong and peculiar smell hanging about the place. They lay there and waited. Barney tried to crawl backwards as far down the hole in the bank as he could.

'That's funny!' he muttered. 'Somebody's put sticks here.' In the mouth of what seemed to be a large rabbit burrow were fixed three stakes of hazelwood, so that no animal that was bigger than a mouse could possibly get in or out. To pass the time, Barney kicked and worried at the stakes until he got them loose, and then cleaned the mud and chalk off them.

'Look, Stig,' he said. 'You could make arrows out of these. Or perhaps they're a bit thick.'

But Stig was not listening. He was looking up the track at an animal the size of a small dog, with reddish fur, sharp ears and very bright eyes, calmly walking towards them with its tongue hanging out.

Barney's heart missed a beat. He got slowly to his feet, gripping his spear.

'Fox!' he hissed. 'That's it, Stig. It really is a fox.' He levelled his hunting spear at the fox, and wished he had the bow and arrows. But perhaps he could spear it.

'Stig!' he breathed. 'Come on, now's your chance.'

But this time Stig did not raise his bow. Instead, he took hold of the end of Barney's spear and held it so that he could not throw it. The fox strolled calmly up to their very feet, gave Stig a glance, and vanished down the hole.

Barney nearly burst into tears of rage. 'But Stig, why did you let him go?' he stormed. 'You're *supposed* to kill foxes. That's what hunting's *for!* That's why we *came!* '

But Stig grinned in a rather superior way. He pointed down the hole after the fox, acted a little pantomime as if he was eating, and screwed up his face as if he was tasting a bad taste. He made it quite clear that he thought Barney was mistaken in wanting to kill something you couldn't eat.

The scufflings in the undergrowth seemed to be just the other side of a bramble patch on the edge of the track.

'Quick, Stig, they're coming!' exclaimed Barney. 'Get back into our hiding place!' And he pulled Stig back into the mouth of the earth. As he did so a large fox-hound came out on to the track and lolloped towards them on the scent of the fox. It came straight for

where they were hiding, looked up and saw Stig, and
bared its teeth and growled.

Stig bared *his* teeth and growled.

The hound looked surprised. It wasn't sure whether
Stig was animal or human, but he was certainly lying
between it and a good strong scent.

The hound took a step forward, making horrible
noises in his throat.

Stig took a step forward on his hands and knees,
making horrible noises in *his* throat.

Barney sat at the back of the little cave, holding his
middle. The hound looked very big and fierce and he
was afraid it might hurt Stig. But then Stig was looking very fierce too, and he might hurt the hound.

Stig was the first to move. With a lightning spring
he darted forward and bit the hound hard on the ear.
It was too much for the poor animal. It was not afraid
of sharp-toothed foxes or other animals that fought

back, but Stig smelt like a man and it had never heard of a man biting a dog. It turned and made off yelping, with its tail between its legs.

Barney looked at Stig. 'I think we better go home,' he said. 'We're supposed to be fox-hunting and what have you done? Killed a pheasant, helped a fox, and

bitten a hound! What are you going to do next, I'd like to know?'

But once again Stig was not listening to Barney. He was hearing something new – the thud and squelch of heavy hooves moving through the woodland glades. And perhaps he was smelling another animal smell. The horses of the hunt followers were moving through the wood, and now at last Stig's face was alight with the excitement of the hunt. Without a sound or a look to Barney, he slipped into the undergrowth and started flitting from thicket to thicket and tree-trunk to tree-trunk towards the sound of the horses, an arrow already strung in his bow and held with his left thumb. Barney followed as best he could through the undergrowth, with a feeling that something had gone badly wrong with his hunting trip, and that something far worse was going to happen any moment.

Stig seemed to pass through the banks of bramble without feeling or caring for scratches, but Barney's mackintosh was always getting caught and ripped, and low branches snatched his hat off, and his rubber boots did not save his knees from scratches, and the more he tried to keep up with Stig the hotter and crosser he was getting. When he came to an open space at last, and saw Stig, and saw what he was doing, all he could do was cover his face with his hands and moan softly to himself: 'Oh, no, no, no, no, no!'

Standing in the track, where the huntsman had left it to go into a thicket on foot, was the huntsman's white horse. Hiding behind a mossy stump, his eyes blazing with excitement, his bow bent to the full, with an arrow pointing straight at the white horse, was Stig.

Stig was really hunting now, and to him, *horses were meat!*

✳

Lou sat on her pony at the edge of the wood. On one side the black trunks of the trees dripped sadly and the wind moaned in the branches, on the other side low ragged clouds swept over the bare stubble fields. Around her were various ladies, gentlemen, and children of the hunt, on bored or fidgety horses, waiting around for something to come out of the wood. They had waited by a field of cabbages and found nothing, they had waited by a field of turnips and seen a hare, they had jogged along lanes and tracks and waited by copses, but they still hadn't found a fox. Lou's cheeks were glowing and so was her nose, her eyes were sparkling, her hair hung down in wet strips, and her numb fingers could hardly feel the reins. Flash, the pony, who in his younger days at least used to live up to his name, stood in a puddle with lowered head and blew steam from his nostrils into the damp air.

'First time out with hounds, young lady?' asked a hearty lady on a big black mare. Lou smiled and nodded and a little shower of drips fell from the peak of her cap.

'Enjoyin' yourself?' asked the lady.

'Yes, thank you. Super!' replied Lou.

All the same, she thought, if only they'd let me go *into* the wood and poke around a bit I'm sure I could find a fox. There must be something going on in there.

At that moment out of the wood came the shrill neighing of an outraged horse. All the waiting horses pricked up their ears, riders nervously shortened their reins, there seemed to be a sort of commotion among the riders that had gone some way into the wood. Horses were backing, rearing, turning in spite of their riders, snorting and neighing. And into the thick of them plunged the huntsman's white horse, riderless, eyes rolling and nostrils wide with alarm, cannoning into horses and riders and sending them sprawling in puddles and mud. It was a stampede. As the huntsman's horse bolted through the middle of them all the other horses whipped round and joined it in mad flight. Most of the riders were caught off balance. Some lost their hats, some lost their reins or stirrups, some lost their seats straight away and were left on the edge of the stubble. Some of them who had been round the corner of the wood thought the fox had gone away and urged their horses after the rest of the field. All Lou could do was stay on top of Flash as best she could and join the stampede. So this was hunting, she thought, though thinking was difficult at full gallop in the middle of a lot of other excited animals. Yet even then she had a feeling that there was something queer. Why wasn't the huntsman on his horse? And had she imagined it or had she seen, sticking into the saddle of the bolting horse, something that looked like an *arrow*?

And Lou was never quite sure whether or not she had seen out of the corner of her eye, at the tail of the hunt, a very odd creature indeed coming whooping out of the wood. Had it been naked and mud-spattered? Did it have hair like a tangled bramble-bush? Did it have rabbit-skins round its middle and a sort of tail of feathers behind? And could it have been brandishing a bow and arrow? No! If one was old enough to go hunting one was really too old to believe in goblins and things. She must have imagined it.

The hunt eventually scattered itself in all directions over the countryside. Riders at last reined in their blown horses and found themselves alone or in small groups in remote stack-yards. They decided they'd had a good day's sport and went home. Nobody was quite sure what happened to the hounds, or the fox, but it had been a good run. Lou, after directing quite a few lost people, got back to her Grandmother's house as the evening was beginning to close in. Barney had got back only a little earlier. They both needed baths and they were both very hungry by the time they sat down to tea in front of a blazing log fire.

'Well,' said Grandmother. 'So you went off hunting after all, Barney!'

'Oo, not *really* hunting like *me*,' said Lou scornfully.

'Well, no,' said Barney, 'I went with Stig, see, and he was only interested in hunting squirrels and pigeons and pheasants really.'

'That's not hunting,' said Lou. 'In England it's only hunting if it's foxes. Or stags.'

'Well, Stig doesn't hunt foxes because they taste nasty. So we let the fox go. But it was so near I could touch it.'

Lou's eyes and mouth were round with disbelief.

'It *was*, Lou, really! And then Stig bit the dog and started hunting the horses. It was jolly funny,' Barney chuckled. 'But I thought I'd better come home.'

Lou looked at Barney very hard, but for once she didn't say anything.

5. The Snargets

'WHY don't you go out and get some fresh air, Barney dear?' asked Grandmother.

Barney stood and looked out of the window. 'Doesn't look very fresh to me,' he grunted. A yellow fog hung over the trees outside. The smoke from the back kitchen chimney stirred itself into it, and there seemed to be a smell of distant cement works.

'Never mind dear, it's better than stuffing indoors all day.'

'All right, Granny, I'll go out.'

After about twenty minutes he had found his jersey mixed up with his bedclothes, one outdoor shoe under the bed and the other one under the chest in the hall. He wandered out into the garden. It was neither warm nor cold and there was no wind at all. He made for the chalk-pit, whistling, and with his hands in his pockets.

As he came near the edge of the pit he stopped whistling, and stood still. There were voices coming from the bottom of the pit. *His* pit!

Well, perhaps it wasn't his pit. It didn't even belong to Grandfather, or did it? Perhaps holes in the ground didn't belong to anybody. All the same, he was quite annoyed that *other people* should be poking around down the pit.

He went cautiously to the edge and peeped over. Down there among the tin cans and other rubbish were three boys of about his own age or older, dressed in jerseys and trousers that were grubbier and more tattered than his own, and grey tennis shoes with holes in the toes. They all had long, rather greasy hair. Barney recognized them. They were the Snarget boys, part of a large family that lived in an old house with tarred weather-boards, and were always 'getting into trouble'. At least, that was what the grown-ups said – but then who *didn't* get into trouble?

The Snargets seemed to be building some sort of shack for themselves out of dead branches and old sheets of corrugated iron, with a lot of horseplay and cries of: 'No, not that way, clever! Like this, see?'

Barney crawled to a place where a twisted tree-trunk grew from the very edge of the cliff, hid himself behind it, broke off a handy-sized clod of clay and roots from the cliff edge, and hurled it at the roof of the shack. It curved through the air towards the target, but missed, and landed almost noiselessly on a mossy log.

Barney chose himself another clod and threw it.

This time it struck the bottom of an upturned pail and exploded like a little bomb, scattering bits of clay over one of the Snargets.

''Ere, 'oo's chuckin' dirt?' cried the first Snarget suspiciously.

'I never,' said another Snarget. 'Must 'ave been 'im,' he added, pointing to the third and youngest.

'Leave off, will yer!' said the first Snarget. 'Or I'll *do* yer, see?'

'I never done nothing!' protested the youngest Snarget.

'Oh, yer didn't, didn't yer?' said the first.

'No I never!'

'Well, don't you do it again, that's all!'

At the top of the cliff, Barney, the cause of the trouble, chuckled to himself and broke off another clod. This time his aim was true, and the clod landed fair and square on the sheet of iron with a most satisfying clang. Three Snarget heads popped out at once like ferrets out of rabbit holes.

'I told yer someone was chuckin' dirt,' said the first Snarget.

'An' *I* told yer it wasn't me,' said the youngest.

They looked round, scowling, at the floor of the pit.

'All right, it's no use 'iding. We can see yer,' called the eldest Snarget.

Barney hugged himself in silence behind his tree trunk. He knew this was just bluff. They hadn't even looked in his direction.

'It's old Albert, I bet,' said the middle-sized Snarget. ''E's been and followed us.'

'We can see yer, Albert,' called the first Snarget. 'Come out of that bush or we'll come and *do* yer!'

They were standing looking at the far end of the pit, with their backs to Barney. With great care, Barney broke off as big a clod as he could find and aimed it again at the roof of the shack. It hit and exploded with another loud clang, scattering pieces over all three Snargets, who ducked wildly and clutched at each other, and then looked foolish at being taken by surprise. They whispered fiercely among themselves, pointing at places on the cliff edge: 'Come from be'ind us, it did! No, up there 'e is! Don't be daft, 'e's up in them bushes. I tell you I *saw* 'im.' They all pointed in different directions at the edge of the cliff.

'It's all right Albert,' called the eldest Snarget again. 'It's no use you 'idin' yerself up there. We're comin' up to *get* yer.' But this didn't worry Barney either. By the time they got to the top, he could be well away. The Snargets must have thought this too, because they didn't make a move. They retired inside their rickety shack instead. Barney scored another direct hit on it and a near miss. Heads popped out each time and looked round fiercely, but he was too well hidden and they failed to spot him. But there seemed to be a lot of whispering going on in the shack, and then all three Snargets came out and started walking towards the way out. The eldest called over his shoulder in a casual voice: 'Good-bye Albert!' and the other two repeated it.

'We're goin' 'ome now Albert,' called the eldest. 'It's our dinner time. But listen 'ere Albert, we know you're up there. Just keep your 'ands off of our shack, see! We got something in there that's *valuable*. We just dare you to meddle with it, that's all!'

The Snargets walked off towards the way out of the pit, whistling loudly and banging tins with sticks. Barney waited until he could hear their feet on the lane, dying away.

Funny, he thought. They've gone. Still, perhaps it *is* their dinner time.

He came out from behind his tree and went round the edge of the pit to the low side, and walked along the bottom to the shack the Snargets had built. He wondered what the valuable thing was they had left in it. There didn't seem to be anything except a paper bag full of chestnut conkers.

'Pooh! Silly old conkers,' said Barney aloud. 'They're not valuable.'

Perhaps they'd buried something. He dug around in the mossy floor and unearthed a very rusty tin box. It had writing on the outside, he could just make out the letters: 'GOLD BLOCK', it said! It felt heavy. Ought he to open it or not? He decided he would. There was no harm in just looking.

The hinged lid was rusted to the bottom and wouldn't move. He banged at it with a stone. Out fell a rusty mass of screws, nuts, bolts, and curtain rings. Inside the lid of the box was more writing which said that Gold Block was the Finest Pipe Tobacco, Made from Choice Virginia Leaf ... Barney threw the tin away in disgust, and a voice said: 'All right mister, come out, we got you covered!'

It was the Snargets! They'd played a trick on him and crept back.

He came out of the shack and faced the Snargets. One had a broken-down old airgun, and the others were pointing sticks.

'Cor! It ain't Albert!' exclaimed the youngest Snarget.

'We can see that!' said the oldest roughly. 'What's yer name?' he said to Barney in the same voice.

'Barney,' said Barney. 'What's yours?'

'I'm the Lone Ranger and 'e's Robin Hood and 'e's William Tell,' snapped the eldest Snarget.

'Golly!' exclaimed Barney.

'Quiet!' snapped the first Snarget. 'What was you doin' in our shack?'

'Yes, and watcher mean by chuckin' dirt at us?' asked the second Snarget.

'Yes, and watcher doin' in our dump anyway?' piped the youngest fiercely.

'Can if I want to,' replied Barney, pretending not to mind. But he was not really feeling very comfortable. He was not sure just how rough these Snargets could get.

' "Can if 'e wants to", 'e says!' exclaimed the Lone Ranger as if he couldn't believe his ears. 'What shall we do wiv 'im, fellers?'

'Tie 'im to a tree and shoot 'im full of arrers,' suggested Robin Hood.

'Put 'im in a dungeon and leave 'im to rot,' said William Tell.

'No, I reckon we ought to lynch 'im on the spot. String 'im up!' said the Lone Ranger masterfully.

'We ain't got no rope,' said Robin Hood.

'Well, we ain't got no bowsanarrers,' pointed out William Tell.

'Well, there certainly ain't no dungeon for miles around,' said the Lone Ranger. 'Let's just give 'im a bit of Slow Torture.'

'You wouldn't dare!' said Barney. But he didn't feel too sure.

'Oh, *wouldn't* we!' sneered the Lone Ranger. 'That's what you think. We often do, don't we fellers? Do it all the time, don't we, give people the Slow Torture?'

'Yes. *And* shoot 'em full of arrers,' agreed Robin Hood.

'*And* put 'em in dungeons,' added William Tell.

'I'd tell a policeman,' said Barney stoutly.

The eldest Snarget looked carefully around the pit. 'Can't see no policeman 'ere,' he said scornfully.

'I'd tell my Granny, and she lives just up there,' said Barney. The Snargets collapsed in howls of laughter.

' 'E'd tell 'is Granny, 'e says! 'Ear that, fellers! 'E'd tell 'is Granny!' they cackled. Barney felt his face going red and tears coming into his eyes. Then he thought of something.

'I'm going to tell Stig,' he said calmly.

The laughter went on. ' 'E's going to tell 'is Stig!' cackled the Snargets, but Barney just stood there and smiled, and the laughter gradually died down.

' 'Oo's Stig?' the eldest Snarget asked suspiciously.

'Oh, a friend of mine,' replied Barney airily.

'Garn, there ain't no such person,' said the second, doubtfully.

'Yes there is. And he's my friend,' said Barney.

'Where's 'e live?' squeaked the smallest Snarget.

'Here,' said Barney.

''*Ere*!' chorused the Snargets scornfully. 'What, in the dump?' jeered the eldest Snarget, and they all laughed as if he had made a joke.

'Yes,' said Barney. 'Didn't you know?'

'Go on! You can't 'alf tell 'em!' said the second. 'What's 'e *do*? Tell us that then!'

'He makes bows out of television aerials and arrows out of bits of flint,' replied Barney. The Snargets gaped at him with open mouths.

'Look 'ere,' said the eldest at last. 'This 'ere Stig of yourn, what *is* 'e then? A boy or a man?'

Barney had to think a little before he answered. Then: 'He's a cave man,' he said.

At once the Snargets burst into jeers and laughter again.

'Yah, soppy old cave man!' ''E's got it out of a school book!' ''E's pullin' our legs. Makin' out he knows a cave man!' 'Come on fellers, let's *do* 'im!' 'Slow torture!' they cried.

But Barney leapt off the pile of rubble he was standing on and set off at a run towards the other end of the pit. The Snargets were after him with shrill cries.

''E's off!'

'Get 'im, fellers!'

'Yah! Chicken! Run away, will yer?'

Barney jumped fallen tree-trunks and burst through banks of nettles without caring for the stings. He knew the bottom of the pit better than the Snargets, and he seemed to be leaving them behind. Then he heard the voice of the eldest: 'Take it easy, fellers. 'E can't get out this end of the pit. Spread out so 'e don't double back!'

But Barney did not mean to double back. As quietly as he could, so that his pursuers could not hear him through the nettle banks and elder trees, he made for the entrance to Stig's den, flung himself through the low doorway, and collapsed, puffing, blowing, and pleased with himself, on the floor of the cave.

Stig was there, busy making himself a really horrible-looking club out of a tree root into which he was fixing bits of flint, broken glass, and rusty nails.

'Hullo Stig!' panted Barney. 'I'm jolly glad to see you.' But when he saw the horrible club he began to feel almost sorry for the Snargets. He couldn't set this monster on to three little boys who hadn't really done anything to him yet. It *may* have been only a game, after all. You never could tell with the Snargets. Barney just smiled uncertainly at Stig, and Stig returned him a friendly grin.

Then from outside came the sound of the Snargets calling to each other: ''As 'e gorn back your way Ted?' 'No. I ain't seen 'im.' 'Must be 'idin' round-about 'ere somewheres.' There were sounds of the undergrowth being beaten and stones being flung into bramble patches. Stig listened and looked at Barney suspiciously, but Barney made signs to be quiet.

'Cor, wait till I get my 'ands on you, Mister Barney, wherever you are!' came the voice of the eldest Snarget. 'I'm all nettle stings one side of me face. We'll roll 'im in the nettles when we get 'im, that's what we'll do.' He sounded as if he meant it, and Barney felt he was not quite so sorry for the Snargets.

Footsteps crackling on dry twigs sounded quite close to the den. Barney moved further back into the cave and made signs to Stig to do the same, but Stig stayed near the entrance, bristling. Suddenly the voice of the youngest Snarget piped up excitedly: 'There's a nole 'ere, a nole! Come out of it!' And a large lump of

chalk came flying in through the entrance and hit Stig smack on the side of the head.

Stig gave one roar and charged out of his doorway. Barney threw himself after him to see what would happen. The youngest Snarget gave one pop-eyed dis- believing look at Stig and turned and fled, sobbing and screaming.

'Aaaaaaoooower! It's a kye – it's a kye – it's a kye – it's a kye – it's a KYVE man!'

The other Snargets, who had been closing in when they heard the youngest's cry of discovery, saw Stig and turned and ran too.

'Wait for me! Wait, wait, don't leave me!' wailed the youngest, and then uttered a shrill scream of terror as he put his foot through the bottom of a rusty enamel basin and fell headlong. 'ELP-ELP-ELP – 'e's-got-me-'e's-got-me-'e's-GOT-ME!!!'

Almost as alarmed as the young Snarget, Barney ran up to where Stig was standing over the boy, who was shivering and moaning with fright and looked as if he expected to be eaten on the spot.

But Stig was standing there looking down at the fallen William Tell Snarget with an almost fatherly look in his eyes. He bent down to help the boy to his feet, and the Snarget moaned feebly: 'Don't, don't.' Then, seeing Barney approaching, he turned his eyes pitifully towards Barney and wailed: 'Don't let 'im 'urt me! Don't let 'im 'urt me! I wasn't doing no 'arm.' But Stig kept hold of him and led him firmly but gently towards his den.

The Snarget gang, trouble-makers though they were, were not as black as they were painted. Anyway, they weren't the men to abandon one of their number to his fate. And perhaps too they had an idea that violence was not always the way to get things done. Stig, Barney, and their captive had not been long inside the den before there came the sound of hesitant footsteps from nearby. Barney looked out, and there were the two other Snargets standing meekly together, unarmed, and holding paper packets in their hands. The middle brother also had a handkerchief, which might have been supposed to be white, tied to a stick.

'We got gifts,' said the one with the white flag.

'Yes,' said the other. 'We come for the little 'un.'

Barney hesitated. 'You better come in,' he said. 'But no tricks!'

'Not likely!' said the middle Snarget. 'Not with that there pal o' yourn about.'

They came in through the doorway, saw Stig for the first time close to, and stopped, their eyes growing rounder and rounder. Then the second of them took a step forward, gingerly, holding out his hand with a paper bag on it.

'For you,' he said in a shaky voice. 'It's jelly-babies.'

Stig took the little bag in a puzzled manner, squeezed it, smelt it, turned it about in his hands. Barney realized that though he was clever at a lot of things he was sometimes surprisingly ignorant about such things as paper bags. Then as he turned the bag in his hairy hands, one jelly-baby fell out on to the floor. Stig's eyes widened and he stooped to pick it up, and held it to the light of the lamp which was flaming in the back of the cave, with a pleased expression on his face. Then he reverently stood the little sweetmeat in a niche in the chalk and stood and looked at it.

'You're supposed to *eat* it, Stig,' said Barney, getting rather tired of this pantomime. 'It's delicious.' He went across to the jelly-baby's little niche and popped it into his own mouth. Stig looked horrified, and Barney was afraid for a moment he was going to hit him.

'There's more in the bag, Stig,' he said hurriedly,

and he took the bag from Stig and opened it and showed him the other little jelly figures. 'Go on, eat one!' he urged.

Stig took one between his finger and thumb, put it slowly in his mouth, and chewed slowly. Barney and the Snargets watched anxiously. Then a smile slowly began to spread over his face. The Snargets, who had been standing there strained and tense, sighed with relief and smiled too. Somehow everyone felt as though some very solemn ceremony had been performed.

Barney handed round the bag and all five of them solemnly ate jelly-babies. Then the middle Snarget produced his second gift, which was little bags of fizzy sherbet with hollow sticks of liquorice stuck in them to suck it through.

They sat down to this. After a little instruction, Stig got the idea of how to suck the fizzy powder up through the little tube, but as soon as he got a mouthful and felt the unusual sensation on his tongue he jumped up with an alarmed expression on his face and began coughing and spluttering, and the Snargets weren't sure whether to laugh or be alarmed too. But Barney banged Stig on the back, which impressed the Snargets even more, and managed to soothe him down again.

Finally, with a flourish, the eldest Snarget produced a packet of Woodbine cigarettes and handed them round. All three Snargets took one as if it was quite a usual thing, but this time it was Barney's turn to hesitate and wonder whether he should. As if he wished to show they were all friends now, Stig took one, beaming, and without even looking to see what the others were doing with theirs, put it in his mouth. The smallest Snarget suddenly exclaimed: ' 'Ere, 'e's eatin' it! ' and before they could do anything, Stig had chewed up the little tube of tobacco and swallowed it with great satisfaction.

The Snargets and Barney lit their cigarettes at the lamp. Barney immediately choked on his and threw it away and decided he didn't like smoking, the smallest Snarget puffed away and turned first white and then green, the other two smoked away quite happily, but Stig, though he ate another one, could not be persuaded to send up in smoke what he considered to be nourishing food.

The Snargets began to feel at home.

' 'E's all right, your pal Stig,' said the eldest Snarget to Barney. ' 'E don't say much though, do 'e? Don't 'e speak English?'

'Smashin' place 'e's got 'ere an' all,' said the second. 'Cor, look at them old spears! '

'I weren't reely feared of 'im,' piped up the youngest. 'I was just makin' out I was.'

'Yes, nor we wasn't reely goin' to do no 'arm to old Barney 'ere, was we fellers? It were all just make believe, weren't it? Reckon old Barney and 'is pal Stig are all right, eh fellers?'

The others agreed in chorus. Barney felt a warm feeling inside now that the Snargets reckoned he and his friend Stig were all right.

'I tell you what,' went on the eldest Snarget. 'Stig an' Barney'll be part of our gang from now on. And we'll all swear an oath we won't none of us tell no one about this 'ere den.'

Barney was going to agree, and then he thought,

well, it was his secret first anyway, so why should he swear about it with anybody?

But the Snargets swore a horrible oath among themselves over the body of the last jelly-baby in the bag, which they then cut the head off and buried to show what would happen to any of them who broke their oath. Barney felt fairly sure that his secret would not spread around the village now, and he felt somehow that Stig and the Snargets would get along very well together.

Barney was quite surprised when he got back to his Grandmother's house to find that he was in good time for lunch and Granny was just dishing up dumplings.

'Did you find something to do outside, dear?' asked his Grandmother. '*Not* a very nice day!'

'I had super fun with the Snargets, Granny. First I bombed them and then they were going to lynch me or torture me or something but I got away to Stig's den and they thought Stig was going to eat one of them but we ate babies instead, you know, jelly ones.'

'Oh!' said Granny. 'Aren't the Snargets rather rough boys for you to play with?'

'Yes, but they're not nearly as rough as Stig. I reckon they're all right,' said Barney.

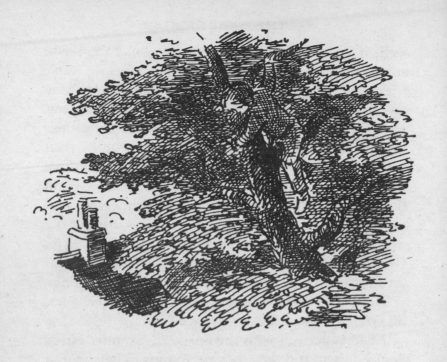

6. Skinned and Buried

BÁRNEY was up the elm tree. It was the one that grew very close to Grandfather's house. It had a swing on one of the lower branches and near the top there was a hole where the jackdaws usually made a nest each year. Barney had climbed up to see how they were getting on this spring, and they had already laid one egg. He climbed higher, among the springy branches at the top, and clung there and let the wind blow him to and fro. He could see the house almost below him, and the garden with a few daffodils and crocuses showing, and the wood and copses where the trees still showed their bones but were beginning to cover them with new green leaves.

He heard Lou's voice somewhere about the house calling for him but he didn't answer. 'I bet she can't find me,' he thought, and grinned to himself. Then he saw his Grandmother and Lou in the yard, going out to the car with shopping-baskets. Grandmother called: 'Barney, where are you?'

Barney chuckled to himself. He could see them, so they could see him if they really looked. But Grandmother and Lou got into the car and drove off, and he could see it going away along the lanes towards the village.

They'd gone off shopping and *left* him! It wasn't *fair*! He was so cross he nearly fell off his branch. Then he thought it was no good trying to stamp your feet when they are wedged in the fork of a branch, and anyhow he might as well stay up here instead of going shopping. He'd really *rather* be up a tree in the wind than go shopping.

He could see ploughed fields with a tractor crawling over the bare earth pulling a harrow. He could see black and white cows on the pasture. He could see chicken houses, and those very very small bits of yellow like grains of sand running about must be baby chicks. He could see a big black car coming along the lane towards the house.

That was funny – it had stopped and pulled off the road into the copse near the chalk-pit.

He could see two men get out and walk towards the house. They wore dark hats and mackintoshes, and didn't look like country people. Had he seen them before?

Yes, he had! They had come to the door once before and he had answered the door-bell. They had asked him if his Grandmother had got any silver or jewels to sell and he had told them that of course Grandmother had lots of silver and jewels but he didn't think she would want to sell them as she'd got some money already. And then Grandmother had come out and told them she didn't want to sell anything thank you and if she did she wouldn't sell it on the doorstep, and she had seemed quite cross. And now the men were coming back again. Well, there was nobody at home and he was going to stay in his tree.

One of the men stayed in the lane and the other went and knocked on the door. Of course nobody answered. The man knocked again and waited a long time. Then he went round to the back door and tried that. It was not locked. The man looked about him, opened the door, and went in.

Barney's heart fluttered and his legs felt funny as if he had nearly fallen off his branch, though he was clinging on with all his might. That man had gone into Granny's house when he *shouldn't* have. He must be a thief! He would take all the silver and drive off with it in his car! And Barney was all alone up in the tree, and though he could see the countryside for miles around he couldn't see a human being except the tractor driver, fields and fields away. There was no one who could help in time.

Yes there was!

Barney started climbing down, trying not to be too shaky and excited. He had to go down the side of the tree that was away from the house, so that he wouldn't be seen, and the best hand-holds and foot-holds were

on the house side. Barney slipped and slithered the
last bit and landed among the bushy twigs that grew
out of the bottom of the trunk. He crouched there for
a few moments, hoping he had not made too much
noise, then he crawled out and ran as hard as he could
across the paddock towards the copse. He scrambled
over the fence and lay among the brambles there,
panting and looking towards the house. He could see
no signs of anyone coming after him, so he got up and
plunged through the copse. Look out, bluebells and
primroses! he thought, I'm in a hurry!

By the time he had got round the down into the pit,
and along the bottom to Stig's cave, he was quite out of
breath.

Stig was there all right. There was a strong smell
coming from something gluey he was melting on the
fire. He was sticking arrow-heads on to their shafts and
binding them with catgut which he was taking from a
broken old tennis racket. He looked all ready for the
spring hunting season.

'Stig!' puffed Barney. 'Thank goodness you're here!
You've got to help! A man's got into Granny's house
and I'm sure he's a thief and he'll take all the silver
and jewels and even my money box if he finds it and
it's got three and threepence in it. What are we going
to do, Stig?'

Stig just grinned in a friendly way and Barney began
to feel hopeless. It was just like when he was trying to
explain about Stig to the grown-ups – they just smiled
and said 'Really?' And of course Stig didn't speak
English. He didn't talk at all much. But he must make
him understand.

'Enemy!' said Barney fiercely, pointing towards the top of the cliff. 'Bad men!' he said, screwing up his face to look wicked. 'Fight 'em Stig, shoot 'em, see 'em off Stig,' he urged, making bow-and-arrow movements and spear movements with his arms.

Stig seemed to get the idea. He grinned more than ever and scowled horribly at the same time. Barney looked around for weapons. Leaning against the wall were a new-looking bow and the arrows Stig had been making, some spears, an axe, and the horrible looking club. Barney picked up the bow and arrows and handed them to Stig, but Stig gave them back to him and took the club instead.

'Can I really have the bowanarrows, Stig?' exclaimed Barney. 'Gosh, thanks! Come on, we've got to be quick!'

They ran out of the far end of the pit and instead of turning right and coming back through the copse to the garden Barney led the way round into the lane and up the hill towards the house. There at the top, where the lane passed near the chalk cliff and there was a gap where lorries backed off the road to dump things over the cliff, they found the big black car parked. And there, coming along the lane, were the two men in raincoats and dark hats, carrying a large suitcase each.

Without thinking, Barney fitted an arrow into the bow and shot it. A dark city hat flipped off the head of one of the men and was pinned to the bank of the lane by a flint-tipped arrow. The men stopped. Then they saw Barney.

'Now then, kid!' said the man. 'Cut it out! That's dangerous, playin' wiv bows and arrers!'

'You're thieves!' said Barney. 'I know, you've got Granny's silver in that suitcase!'

The man looked at his companion. ''Ear that?' he said. 'The kid thinks we're thieves. Look, sonny, we come to look at your Granny's television, didn't we, Sidney? We got our tools in these 'ere cases, 'aven't we, Sidney?'

'That's right,' said Sidney.

'Plucky little nipper though, ain't e', Sidney? Lookin' after 'is Granny's 'ouse while she's away, eh sonny? I got some toffees for you in the car.'

'I don't like toffees,' said Barney. But he was beginning to feel foolish, and he lowered his bow, which he was pointing at the man with another arrow fitted.

The man turned round for his hat, which had the arrow stuck through it. He pulled the arrow out, then he looked at the sharp flint tip and his face went white.

'You little 'orror!' he snarled at Barney. 'Where'd you get them things from, eh? You know you might 'ave *killed* me?' He broke the arrows across twice and threw the pieces angrily on the ground. 'Come on!' he said. ''And over the rest of them things! OR there'll be trouble!' He came towards Barney with a very nasty expression on his face.

Stig had been lurking behind the car, listening to the strange talking and wondering what it was all about. When he saw the man break his precious arrow and come angrily towards Barney it was enough for him. He let out a sound that was something between a growl and a howl and dashed at the man, raising his horrible club. The two men took one look at this wild figure, dropped their suitcases, and ran, with Stig in mad pursuit and Barney running after Stig.

'Stig! Stig! Come back!' shouted Barney. 'It's all a mistake. They're not bad men! They're not thieves, they came to mend the television!' But it was no use. What did Stig know about television?

There was a barbed-wire fence at the top of the lane and the men decided to get over it in the hope of escaping from Stig. As the second one scrambled over, his raincoat got caught in the wire. In a panic, he struggled out of the coat and ran off over the field, leaving it on the fence. It was this that saved him from the teeth of Stig's club, because Stig stopped to look at the coat, as if he was not quite sure what part of himself the man had left behind. Barney caught up with him and took hold of his arm.

'Stig! Stig! You mustn't chase those men,' Barney panted. 'I thought they were thieves but they're not. They might tell a policeman and then there'll be awful trouble.'

But Stig was looking at the coat. As he turned it about there was a tinkling sound, and a whole lot of shining things fell out of a pocket on to the ground. Stig pounced on them with wide-open eyes, picked them up and admired them, turning them to the light.

'No, Stig,' said Barney. 'You can't have them. They're only the man's teaspoons. I expect he was going to have a picnic. Hey, just a *minute*!'

Barney pulled Stig by the arm. 'Come on!' he urged. 'We'd better look at those suitcases.'

They ran back down the lane to where the suitcases were lying. Barney opened one of them.

'Golly!' he exclaimed. All Granny's spoons and forks and ladles and things, her jewels and trinkets from her dressing table, one pair of cuff-links belonging to Grandfather, *and* his own money-box! He shook the money-box. Did it still sound like three shillings and threepence?

So they were thieves after all! What should he do now? They might come back to their big black car any time and drive away. How could he stop them? He ran to the car, opened the rear door, and looked inside. Under some sacks were more suitcases and bags that clanked when he felt them. Loot from other people's houses!

Barney sat in the front seat and held the steering wheel. If only he could drive he could take the car to the police. He took off the hand brake – at least he knew how to do that. The car began to roll backwards – towards the edge of the pit! In a panic, Barney opened the door and scrambled out, with the car still moving. Barney's mouth was open and he held his middle as he watched the big black car move slowly towards the pit. There was a lurch as first one back wheel, then another, went over the edge. The car bumped down on its underneath: perhaps it would stop now. But no, the edge of the chalk crumbled, the rear of the car settled lower, the front wheels rose slowly in the air, and with a horrible scraping and grinding the whole car slid over the edge. There seemed to be quite a long time before Barney heard the crash as the car hit the bottom of the dump, but he felt too sick to look.

When he opened his eyes he saw Stig looking over the edge of the cliff, waving and pointing and grinning all over his face as if it were some great animal they had just hunted over the cliff and he was looking forward to cutting up the meat. Then he was running off round the pit to get to the bottom.

Barney remembered the suitcases, and hurriedly hid them deep in a bramble patch before running off after Stig again. By the time he got to the car, which was lying on its back with its wheels in the air, Stig was already hard at work skinning the leather off the seats and the carpets off the floors. Barney stood helplessly watching. Stig obviously thought that anything thrown into his dump was for him to do what he liked with. But if the men came back and found them at it they would be very angry. Then he saw what they would have to do.

He got up on the pile of rubbish at the foot of the cliff and started throwing things on top of the dead motor-car – old wash-tubs, bedsteads, bicycle frames. Stig soon got the idea – they were burying the animal to hide it from the enemy. Before long the car was covered with bits and pieces, branches and moss.

Then, as they worked, Stig suddenly froze into stillness, and listened. Barney listened too. There were voices coming from the top of the cliff. Barney crept into the inside of the upturned car and beckoned Stig in too. They crouched on the ceiling, looking up at the seats and pedals, and listened.

The voices of the two men came down from the top of the cliff.

'Well it ain't there, is it? Go on, 'ave a good look!'

'All right then, it's gone. What do we do now?'

'We got a nice long walk, that's what we've got, mate. Or if yer don't like walkin', yer can run. Yer seem to like runnin' all right.'

''Oo likes runnin'? You run too, didn't yer?'

'You started runnin' first. Got windy because a couple of kids was playin' Red Indians, so we've lost the lot, all through you.'

'I tell you they wasn't kids. One wasn't, anyways.'

'What was it then?'

'It was a Fing, I tell yer. An 'orrible Fing. Out of that there pit I shouldn't wonder. Come on, let's get out of 'ere. I tell yer I don't like this place. I'm gettin' back to town, if I have to walk all the way.'

Barney smiled at Stig as the voices faded away. Stig grinned and shook his horrible club.

*

Granny and Lou were back from shopping when Barney struggled in through the front gate carrying the two heavy suitcases full of silver.

'Barney, what on earth have you been up to?' Granny exclaimed.

'I've brought your spoons and forks back, Granny. You see two men came to do the television. I mean that's what they said, but they were thieves really and I was up the tree but me and Stig chased them away and I let their car go over into the chalk pit, and it's there now with all the treasure in it.'

'Well, you *have* been having fun,' said Granny. 'Now's let's have tea, shall we. Lay the table Lou, and Barney, go and wash your hands. Look at them!'

Lou started laying the table. 'Where are the teaspoons, Granny?' she asked.

'In the usual place I suppose dear,' said Granny from the kitchen. Barney put his hand to his mouth.

'No they're not, Granny, he said. 'They're hanging on the fence in Mr Tickle's field.'

'What!' Granny exclaimed. 'Really, Barney, that's naughty. You know you mustn't take the silver for games.'

'I didn't take them, Granny,' Barney protested. 'It was the television man, and Stig was running after him with a club and I tried to stop him because I thought he wasn't a thief, but he took his coat off and left it hanging on the fence and the spoons fell out. I thought he was going to have a picnic at first but then I knew they were yours. I'll go and fetch them.' And he ran out.

When Barney got back there was a policeman at the door talking to Granny. She looked worried.

'What's this about thieves, sonny?' asked the policeman.

'Yes, I saw them up the tree, I mean *I* was, and one of them went into the house, and I went to fetch my friend Stig, and me and Stig had a fight with them and they ran away and the teaspoons fell out and the car was full of treasure.'

The policeman scratched his head. 'Ah now, a *car*, you say. Just where might this car be?'

Barney stood on one leg. 'Well, I thought perhaps I could drive it to the police station, but it went backwards over the cliff and Stig thought it was dead and started skinning it and then we buried it. But I couldn't *help* it, I *promise*!'

The policeman was trying to write all this down in a notebook, but when he got to the part about skinning and burying the car he stopped writing and looked hard at Barney.

'You wouldn't be making this up, would you son?' he asked sternly.

'I'm afraid my grandson has a very strong imagination,' said Granny.

'But I'm telling the truth, Granny! I *promise*!' said Barney.

'Perhaps the little boy would like to show me where this, er, alleged treasure is, ma'am,' suggested the policeman.

'Yes, yes!' cried Barney. 'It's just down the lane. Come on!' And he took the policeman by the hand and pulled him through the front gate, and down the lane, explaining as he went.

'It's all in the bottom of the car, the treasure. Or,

well, it's in the top of the car I suppose because the car's upside down in the bottom of the pit.'

He led the way to the top of the cliff where the car had gone over and pointed. 'It's down there,' he said.

The policeman looked over. 'I can't see nothing,' he said.

'Of course not,' explained Barney. 'We buried it. Come on down and see.'

The policeman looked more and more disbelieving. 'Look, son,' he said. 'There's three houses been burgled in the district, and it's my job to catch the thieves and get the valuables back. And I haven't got a lot of time to waste. What about this treasure of yours?'

'It's *down* there,' Barney insisted. 'I'll show it to you if you just come down.'

He led the way round the top of the pit to the way in. It was getting dark now, and the policeman took an electric torch from his pocket. They clambered over the heap of rubbish, and Barney moved aside the branches that hid the door of the upturned car.

'In there!' he said.

The policeman shone his torch inside. There was a terrible mess of ripped leather, broken glass from the windows, scattered stuffing from the seats, and bare springs. No sign of the treasure.

The policeman sat down on an old wash-tub and took his helmet off. He looked quite like an ordinary man.

'What's your name, son?' he asked, quite kindly.

Barney told him.

'Listen to me, young Barney,' said the policeman. 'When I was a youngster I used to have what your Granny calls a strong imagination too. Used to play cops and robbers, and I can tell you it was a lot more exciting and a lot more fun than being a real copper, which I am now. So I'm not blaming you – understand, You *imagined* you had a fight with two robbers, see? You *imagined* this bit of old junk what's been here for years was a car that went over the cliff. Isn't that it? You wasn't telling lies, because you thought it was true. But that's it, isn't it? It never really happened, eh?'

Barney stood there dumbly. If a grown-up said so, and such a kind grown-up, and a policeman too, perhaps you could imagine fights with robbers and cars going over cliffs. Perhaps he just *imagined* Stig. He was looking miserably into the darkness of the pit and was just about to nod his head and agree with all the policeman was saying when he saw in the far corner of the pit a flicker of light. Stig's den!

He scrubbed away some tears that had got into his eyes and said firmly: 'It *did* happen. And I know where the treasure is.' And he went scampering away along the gloomy bottom of the pit towards the den.

He knew his way pretty well now, even in the dark, but as he went he kicked cans and rattled old sheets of iron as much as he could. He wanted to give Stig warning that they were coming. He felt it would be too much, trying to explain Stig to the policeman, even if Stig was there in front of his eyes. He heard the policeman coming along behind him, making even more noise, and he was almost sure he heard a scuffle and a rustle that was Stig hiding himself in his favourite bramble patch. When he got to the entrance to the den, well ahead of the policeman, there was no sign of Stig in the bright firelight inside.

He stood by the entrance and waved the policeman in. The policeman doubled himself up and crawled in through the low entrance. Then he gasped.

It looked like Aladdin's cave. Necklaces and bracelets hung winking from the roof of the shelter. The floor of the cave was carpeted with the skin of the car seats. Stig's bed was made up with padding from the seats and covered with fur coats, and above it, stuck into the wall, was a driving mirror and a set of switches and buttons saying 'HEADLIGHTS' and 'WIPER' and 'HEATER'. And all round the floor, stuck into the ground and set out like tin soldiers on parade, were troops of silver spoons and forks. Stig *had* been enjoying himself!

'Well, I'm blest!' exclaimed the policeman. He took out his notebook. 'I take it all back, Barney, me boy. And if you'll just help me tick off in my book all this stolen property which *someone* has so kindly put out on parade for us, we'll get it back to its rightful owners all the quicker. And I shouldn't be surprised if there was a reward for a bright boy at the end of all this.'

Barney started to explain all over again what had happened, but the policeman said he'd had a tiring day and he'd rather not have any more explanations.

But that time, when he went home from his Grandmother's house, he took a brand-new bicycle with him. And Stig? Well, Stig was disappointed at not being allowed to keep all the treasure, but before he went, Barney found some spanners in the wreck of the car and he taught Stig how to use them. Stig was very proud of his necklace of steel nuts strung on wire cable, and his bangles of piston rings.

7. Party Manners

It was the Easter holiday. Barney and Lou were doing some painting in the dining-room and Granny had spread some sheets of newspaper over the table in case they made a mess. Barney had his elbows on the table and was reading the newspaper.

'Hey, Lou!' he suddenly cried. 'Look what it says here. It says "BOTTOM'S MAMMOTH CIRCUS". D'you think we can go to it?'

'I expect it's an old newspaper,' said Lou, without looking up from the horse she was drawing. 'The circus has probably been and gone a long time ago.'

'No, but Lou, do come and see,' begged Barney. It might not have.'

Lou came round the table and looked at the

advertisement. ' "WORLD'S GREATEST TRAVELLING SHOW," ' she read. 'Golly! Liberty horses, Ranji and his elephants, Daring Wild Animal Act.'

'Yes, but Lou, when *is* it?' said Barney impatiently.

'Wait a minute. Opens at Maidsford, April 17. That's next week! Come on Barney, let's ask Granny if we can go!'

But when they bounced into the drawing room their Grandmother was sitting in a chair talking to a strange lady. This sort of thing was unusual enough in Granny's house. They stood in the doorway goggling until their Grandmother said: 'Come and say how-do-you-do to Mrs Fawkham-Greene children!' They came in and shook hands.

'These are my grandchildren, Barney and Lou,' explained Grandmother to the strange lady. 'They're staying with me for part of the holidays.'

'But how *nice* for you!' cooed Mrs Fawkham-Greene. 'And such bonny children too! I do wish I had known about them. I'm giving a fancy-dress party for my little niece on Wednesday. Do you think Barney and Lou would like to come? Most children nowadays seem to hate parties, but I think they're good for them, don't you?'

'Oo, a fancy-dress party!' exclaimed Lou. 'Do let's go Granny! I'll go as a puma!'

'And I'll be a cave man!' said Barney. 'Granny, can we? And Granny, can we go to the circus too? It's next Monday. Please Granny, let's!'

'Now, now, now!' exclaimed Granny. 'Circuses and cave men and pumas! I'm afraid we'll have to see, dears.'

'They do seem to be keen, the darlings,' said Mrs Fawkham-Greene. 'Do bring them if you can, I'm sure they'd look charming as a puma and a cave man. My little niece is going to be a Dresden shepherdess. We got the costume specially from London, and she looks *so* sweet in it. It's been so delightful meeting your charming grandchildren. I do hope we shall be seeing them on Wednesday.'

Mrs Fawkham-Greene swept out and drove off in a large shiny car, and Granny began to explain the difficulties of making fancy-dress costumes with only a day and a half to do it in. *Perhaps* they could go to the circus instead of the party, but she thought their parents were coming at the week-end to take them home.

The children went off rather gloomily. They hadn't the heart to go on painting. Lou curled up with an animal story book: Barney stood by the window and thought.

Then without a word Barney slipped out of the house. When he got to the middle of the back lawn he stopped and thought again. He went back into the house, crept upstairs, and searched around his bedroom until he found his precious collection of glass marbles, then he slipped out of the house again and set off for the chalk pit.

He was wondering if the plan he had thought of would work. Or rather he hadn't got a plan – he just had a feeling that Stig could help him once more. But it was going to be difficult to explain this time. He was sure that Stig wouldn't understand about fancy-dress parties. But Stig had such a lot of things in his den that some of them were bound to come in useful – if he could get Stig to part with them.

When he got to the den he found Stig happily peeling an old umbrella somebody had thrown away down the pit. He ripped the cover off and tried it on himself in different ways. By tearing a bigger hole in the middle and climbing into it he found it made quite a useful sort of skirt.

'That's clever, Stig!' exclaimed Barney. 'It'll keep the rain off too.'

Stig then turned his attention to the frame of the umbrella. He wrenched the little struts off one by one, and then sat looking at them as they lay in a heap in front of him. Barney could tell he was wondering what he could use them for. He found the first use without thinking – it was just right for scratching an itch in the middle of his back. He looked at another one for some time and played with it in his hands. He found that he could stick its two legs into the ground so that the long part reached forward at an angle. Suddenly he reached for a small turnip and stuck it on the end that was in the air. The whole thing wobbled a bit, so he fitted another strut so that there were four legs to hold up the turnip. Then he brought it near the fire so that the turnip was hanging over the hot embers – and there it was, a standing toasting-fork, or spit. Stig played with another of the pieces of metal and bent it with his strong hands so that one of the ends snapped off. So then he had a thin piece of metal with a hole in the end. It was not long before he had rubbed the other end to a point on a rough stone – and there was a useful big needle.

Stig seemed very pleased with all the things he could do with his bits of umbrella. He put the other metal parts aside, broke off the handle, which was carved like a Scottie-dog, and stuck that into the wall as a decoration, and put the handle of the umbrella against the wall with his weapons. It would make a good arrow.

Barney had been so fascinated, watching Stig inventing uses for the bits of umbrella, that he had almost forgotten what he had come for. Then he remembered about the fancy-dress party. He put his hand into his pocket, and took out a glass marble.

'I brought this for you, Stig,' he said.

Stig took the marble with interest, held it up to the light, grinned, and put it in his mouth.

'No, no, Stig!' cried Barney. 'It's not for eating. Spit it out, Stig, please!'

Stig took the marble out of his mouth and looked at Barney questioningly.

'It's just for playing with,' explained Barney. 'Look, here's another!' He rolled the second marble along the ground to Stig. Stig seemed amused at the way the little glass ball rolled around, flashing in the light. He rolled his marble at Barney's, and they struck and bounced apart. He played with both of them for a bit, and then handed them back to Barney.

'No, they're for you, Stig,' said Barney. 'You can keep them.' Stig put them carefully in a niche in the wall and then seemed to look about for something to give Barney in exchange. He picked up two or three of his precious umbrella-bones and offered them to Barney, but Barney pushed them away.

'No thank you, I don't think I want bits of umbrella,' he said. Stig looked relieved. He didn't really want to part with them. He went to a pile of metal things and came back with a brass bedstead-knob and offered it to Barney. Still Barney shook his head, hoping that Stig would not be offended if he kept on refusing things. He had his eye on a pile of skins in the corner, and Stig seemed to notice this, for he went across to it and picked up a sort of apron of rabbit-skins stitched together, just like what he usually wore himself.

Barney's face lit up. 'Can I have that, Stig? Oo, thank you!' He took the skins under his arm.

There were a lot more skins in the pile. Barney squatted down and turned them over. There were mole-skins, squirrel-skins, things that looked like cat-skins, and they made Barney wonder how they got there. Then he gave a gasp of surprise. Near the bottom was the skin of a great animal, head and all, and it was golden and spotted with black. A leopard! Barney dragged it out and goggled at it. 'Gosh, Stig! Did you kill this?' he asked.

Stig looked at him.

Barney made spearing movements at the skin, put a questioning expression on his face, and pointed to Stig. Stig grinned and shrugged his shoulders. He seemed to be willing that Barney should think he had killed a leopard, but Barney was rather suspicious. He had seen leopard-skins like this worn by soldiers in military bands, and he *had* seen them on floors in people's houses. Perhaps someone had just thrown this one away. It was amazing what people *did* throw away, you only had to look around the dump and in Stig's cave to see that sometimes they were quite valuable. Anyhow, there was the leopard-skin, and Lou wanted to go to the party as a leopard, or was it a puma? She ought to be quite satisfied with this leopard anyway. There were only a few patches where the hair was falling out. But would Stig want to part with it?

Barney felt in his pocket. He had only spent two marbles so far, and he had quite a lot more. He took out two more, held them out to Stig, and pointed at the leopard-skin.

Stig looked at the marbles, looked at the skins, and looked very doubtful.

Barney added another marble to the two in his hand.

Stig still looked doubtful.

Barney took two more marbles from his pocket. Now there were five.

Suddenly Stig seemed to understand that Barney had quite a pocketful of marbles to spend. He held out both hands to Barney, with all the fingers spread out. 'Ten! A leopard-skin costs ten marbles,' thought Barney. He hoped he had that many. He put the first five marbles on the ground and counted out what was left in his pocket. Six, seven, eight, nine – there were three more.

'Here, you might as well have them all,' said Barney, and handed over all twelve. Stig had been checking the marbles on his fingers while Barney counted. When he found he had more marbles than fingers he was so delighted that he went to another corner of the cave and came back with a stone axe on a wooden handle and gave it to Barney with the skin.

'Golly, Stig, can I have that as well?' exclaimed Barney. He was delighted too. 'Oh, Stig, you are kind to let me have all these things. Thank you, *thank* you! I've got to go now, Stig, and show Lou what we've got. We'll be able to go to the fancy-dress party now. Good-bye!'

And Barney danced out, clutching the two bundles of skins and the stone axe.

When he got back to the house he had an idea. He took the bundles quietly to his own room, undressed except for his underclothes, and after some struggles with a couple of safety-pins, got himself dressed in the rabbit-skins. He looked at himself in the mirror and scowled fiercely. But there was something missing. Bother! He had had a haircut only two weeks ago and he didn't have nearly enough hair. He had another idea. He crept downstairs to the broom cupboard and took the head off a mop. When he tried it on his own head in front of the mirror it looked just right. He found a way of tying it under his chin so it stayed there.

He took his axe in one hand and the leopard-skin in the other and crept along the passage to his sister's room. As he expected, she was still lying on her bed with a book. He gave a whoop and charged into the room, waving his axe.

Lou jumped like a startled cat and faced Barney furiously. 'You're not to frighten people like that when they're not expecting it!' she said angrily. 'I knew it was you, Barney.'

'Oh no you didn't,' chuckled Barney. 'Anyhow I'm not Barney, I'm Stog – Stig's brother.' And he did a war dance round the bedroom.

'Where have you been?' asked Lou, more calmly.

'Me? Me been hunting,' said Barney. 'Look what I killed!' And he threw the leopard-skin on the floor. Lou's eyes nearly popped out of her head. 'Golly, Barney, where did you get that?' she said.

'Killed it in the wood,' boasted Barney.

'No, tell me honestly, Barney, please!'

'Well, I didn't really kill it, I was just pretending,' said Barney. 'I got it from Stig.'

'Oh, *Stig*!' scoffed Lou. 'You and your Stig! You mean you found it in the dump?'

'I got it from Stig, I tell you,' repeated Barney. 'And you owe me twelve marbles. You needn't have it if you don't want it.' And he snatched it away.

'No, no, *please* Barney, let me have it. It's a lovely leopard-skin. I'll get you some marbles next time we go into town. Come on, help me try it on!'

Between them, with the help of pins and strings, they managed to dress Lou in the leopard-skin. The bare patches hardly showed and it didn't really smell any more than a real leopard would. And once Lou was inside the skin she became more like a big cat than any leopard had ever been. She wrinkled up her nose and spat, she slunk and clawed. They hunted each other in and out of the bedrooms and along the passages, and then Lou said, 'Pretend I'm a tame leopard and you're my master, and we live in this cave.' And they crept under Lou's bed and curled up.

Barney said, 'Look, Lou, about this party on Wednesday. I know where the house is, just through the woods. We needn't even ask Granny to take us, we'll just go . . .'

*

One or two stars had come out in the dark blue sky overhead and there was a golden wash of sunset in the

west, above the dark woods. A blackbird was trying out his new spring voice from the elm tree. It had been the first mild dry day of spring and the air was beginning to feel alive with the earth warming up, and buds opening, and things creeping out of their winter beds. A leopard and a stone-age hunter, as they let themselves quietly out of the back door, felt they couldn't possibly have stayed indoors any longer without bursting.

The leopard dropped to hands and feet as soon as it reached the lawn, but the hunter said, 'Oh, come on Lou, we'll be late if you're going to crawl all the way!'

'I can go just as fast like this,' said the leopard, and went bounding off towards the back gate. As they let themselves into the paddock, Flash the pony pricked up his ears, snorted, and went careering round the paddock in alarm and excitement. 'Silly old Flash!' called the leopard. 'It's only me.'

'I thought you were a leopard,' said Barney. 'So did Flash. No wonder he's frightened!'

They made their way along darkening tracks and footpaths. Sometimes the leopard would go ahead and leap out from behind a bush at the hunter: sometimes the hunter would run on and lie in wait for the leopard.

One time when Barney was lying in ambush behind a hollow beech-stump, Lou crept up behind him and jumped on *him* instead of coming along the path and being jumped on. Barney was cross. 'That's not fair,' he complained. 'It's my turn to do *you*.'

But Lou only laughed in a catty sort of way and went bouncing off ahead again. Barney sat down rather sulkily and let her go on. He should have had another turn, he thought. He heard Lou's footsteps dying away along the track and then suddenly there was the snarl and roar she usually gave when she was ambushed. It sounded rather astonished this time. Then he heard Lou's voice: 'Barney, it was *my* turn for an ambush. How did you get ahead so quickly?'

But he hadn't gone ahead! He'd been sitting here. Who was Lou talking to, and what was going on?

He got up and ran along the path between the dark thickets. He found Lou a good distance ahead, crouching down and panting.

'You did make me jump that time,' said Lou. 'I wasn't expecting you. How did you get there so soon?'

'Get where?' asked Barney, wondering.

'Behind that oak tree. I know it was you all right, but I wasn't expecting you,' said Lou.

'But I wasn't behind that oak tree. I was along the path there,' said Barney.

'Oh don't be silly, Barney. I saw you with my own eyes didn't I?' said Lou crossly. 'You must have been there.'

'But I wasn't. I *promise*,' Barney protested. 'How could I have *got* there?'

Lou said nothing for a moment, then in a different voice she said, 'I think we'd better stop playing this game. We'll only be late for the party. Let's just walk on.'

They went on side by side. The wood was getting really dark now, and as they went along by the fir plantation the leopard and the hunter actually found themselves holding hands.

'You know people say they sometimes have a feeling someone's following them?' Lou suddenly said in a voice that tried to be bright and ordinary.

'What about it?' said Barney.

'Oh nothing,' said Lou. 'I suppose it's not far now to the Fawkham-Greenes'.'

But Barney had suddenly had an idea. Lou had seen something behind an oak tree, looking like him. And now there was this feeling of being followed. Barney thought he knew what *was* going on. But Lou didn't. And he laughed softly to himself.

'I don't see there's anything to *laugh* at,' snapped Lou almost tearfully, and she stamped her foot.

They came out at last into the lane, crossed over, and there was the entrance to the Fawkham-Greenes' drive. They could see cars parked outside the house, big ones and little ones, and lights blazed from the windows and from over the front door. Lou's eyes began to sparkle, but now Barney started to feel uncomfortable. He liked parties almost as much as Lou, once they had started, but he felt shy about going up to the big door and ringing the bell. As Lou skipped up the steps and pulled the handle, Barney took a grip on his axe and looked back along the shadowy drive. And yes! He was almost sure! Something had slipped between two rhododendron bushes. It was what he had thought. Someone *was* lurking behind them. It was Stig!

The front door opened and Mrs Fawkham-Greene stood there looking a little distracted already.

'Hullo, *do* come in,' she cried. 'Oh, it's the puma and the cave man, how sweet of you to come, and how *realistic*!' She sniffed a little at the animal smell that came in with them, but there was a wail from behind her and she had to turn round to the mass of children of all ages who were hurtling about the big hall or standing dumbly in corners. 'Oh dear, who is it behind the mask there, Lone Ranger or is it Zorro? Please don't poke Little Bo-Peep with your sword, will you, dear? She's only three and she doesn't like it.'

Lou looked round excitedly at the dressed-up chil-

dren. There were peasant girls and ladies from the
Middle Ages and cowboys and kings and queens and
cowboys and a space-man who was looking rather hot
already and more cowboys and Indians and squaws,
but she seemed to be the only one in a real animal
skin. Barney was looking at the walls of the hall.

'Look at all those things on the wall, Lou!' he
whispered. There was hardly a square foot of the wall
that was not covered with trophies: heads of gazelles
and hartebeest and gnus, bunches of spears and asse-
gais and leather shields, racks of swords and daggers
and old guns. 'This is a super place,' murmured Barney. 'I'm jolly glad we came, aren't you?'

Mrs Fawkham-Greene clapped her hands loudly. 'Now then, children!' she called. 'I think we're all here, so we'll start off by dancing Sir Roger de Coverley. I expect you all know it, don't you? The girls do anyway, and they can show the boys.'

Most of the girls began twittering with pleasure, and formed themselves in line ready to begin. But there were glum looks among the boys, and they stood around grasping various weapons. It was going to be *that* sort of party, was it?

'Come on, boys, line up! All pistols, tomahawks, ray-guns, and stone axes on the oak chest, if you please,' carolled Mrs Fawkham-Greene, as she sat down at a big grand piano. The boys lined up sheepishly and the music began, and the girls hopped and skipped and the boys blundered and bumped, and everyone was rather glad when the dance came to an end.

Mrs Fawkham-Greene had got everything well organized. After the dancing they had guessing games, and acting games, and sitting-in-a-ring games, and she had just handed out pieces of paper and pencils to everyone who could write, and got one of the older girls to do ring-a-ring-o'-roses with the tinies when – all the lights went out!

'The fuses!' wailed Mrs Fawkham-Greene. 'One of you older ones get a game going, will you? I won't be long, I hope.' And she made her way into the back part of the house.

There was a lot of scuffling and squeaking in the dark, only lit by the flickering flames from the big fireplace. Of course it had to be Lou who thought of something.

'We'll have a leopard-hunt,' she said. 'Give me twenty to get away, and you've all got to hunt me and put me in a cage. All right?'

There were shouts of agreement, boys scrambled for their weapons in the dark, several people counted up to twenty, everybody shouted 'Coming', and except for a few tiny ones who stayed by the fire, everyone scattered up the stairs and along corridors, whooping and chattering and telling each other to be quiet.

Barney was one of the first up the broad staircase and on to the dark landing. Moonlight came in through a leaded window and shone on a figure standing there. He was just going to say something to it when he noticed it was an empty suit of old-fashioned armour. But there *was* someone coming up the stairs close behind him. He saw the head-dress of the Indian Chief. 'Seen the leopard?' asked the Indian.

'No,' said Barney. 'Let's go along here.'

They went along the corridor and at the end there was a bare wooden staircase going up and down. 'Come on up!' said the Indian. They climbed the stairs, their feet making quite a noise on the bare boards, and found themselves almost at the top of the house. There was an un-lived-in feeling up there. The Indian tried the door of a room, and it opened. There was nothing but boxes and trunks in the room, and there was a big window through which the moonlight came.

'That leads on to the roof, that window,' said the Indian. 'I know, I've been there.'

'Perhaps she's on the roof. The leopard I mean,' said Barney.

'Might be,' said the Indian. He struggled to open

113

the window. They both got through it and out on to a ledge with a parapet. The roof sloped up behind them. They leaned over the parapet and looked a long way down to the moonlit lawn.

And there, in the middle of the lawn, an animal was crouching. Barney's heart gave a bump although he knew he was only hunting for his sister. 'Look!' he gasped to his friend the Indian. 'There it is, the leopard. Down there!'

'Crumbs!' exclaimed the Indian. 'Doesn't it look real! Come on, down again, quick!'

They got back in through the window, bumped through the box-room, clattered down the stairs, and made for the main staircase, calling out: 'Outside, everybody. The leopard's in the garden. Everybody out!' Hunters who had been crawling under beds and giggling in closets and wardrobes made for the staircase too, and the big door was left open and they all streamed out into the moonlit garden.

'In the shrubbery!' shouted Barney. 'Leopard's in the shrubbery! Let's drive it out!' Pirates, cowboys, and shepherdesses piled into the shrubbery, whooping and crashing, and out of the corner of his eyes Barney saw something bolt out of the undergrowth and into the shadow of the house. 'Tally-ho! he hallooed, and sped after it along the gravel path and round the back, past glasshouses and outbuildings. He heard running feet behind him: the Indian and some other hunters were on the trail too.

In front of him were two big wooden gates, open, and leading into a paved stable yard with buildings all round it. 'In there!' he panted. 'I saw it go.' He dashed through the gateway, and at least half a dozen others clattered in with him. 'Quick! Shut the gates! Don't let it get out!' he heard the Indian say, and the heavy wooden doors banged to behind him. But Barney stood rooted to the pavement, unable to move.

The other children behind him were suddenly still and silent too. The boy dressed as the Indian gave a shaky whisper: "There – there's two leopards!'

The moonlight shone clearly on the roofs of the buildings and the chequered paving of the yard. And clearly in the moonlight, like two figures on a stage, two animal forms crouched facing each other. Both had golden, black-spotted fur and long tails. But as one of the crouching beasts turned its head to glare at the hunters by the gate, its eyes flashed green and alive in the moonlight. And under the mask of the other beast Barney recognized the white face of his sister.

How long they all stood like that, Barney didn't know – Barney grasping his stone axe but feeling as if he was turned to stone himself, Lou crouched there, desperately willing her whole body to turn into a real live wild beast to meet this awful peril, and the real live leopard itself – because it couldn't be anything else – frightened by the hullabaloo, mystified by the strange half-beast half-human that faced it, cornered and angry. It was like a nightmare game, when nobody knew what the next move should be.

And then Barney heard the Indian behind him give another hoarse whisper: 'Two cave men!'

For out of the shadows at the far end of the yard appeared a figure that might have been his own reflection in a mirror: shaggy hair, rabbit-skins, and bare limbs. But this one carried a long spear with a glinting blade, and it was levelled at the real leopard. And suddenly Barney's limbs unfroze, and he whispered, 'Stig!'

The leopard shifted its gaze. It shot a glance at Barney. It looked back at the unmoving Lou. It turned to the advancing Stig and gave a low growl. Its tail twitched and it began tucking its feet under it as a cat does when it is about to charge and spring. Stig crouched too, still pointing his spear. And Barney saw that in the shadows beyond Stig was the open door of an empty stable.

The leopard had decided which was its most dangerous enemy and now kept its eyes on Stig. Barney crept forward behind it. He was almost within axe-reach of its twitching tail.

The leopard stopped shifting its feet. Its tail lay
still for an instant. Its muscles were tense. It sprang,
but as it sprang Barney brought his axe down on the
tip of its tail, Lou burst into life with a sudden roar,
Stig threw himself sideways, and the startled and con-
fused leopard jumped twice as high and twice as far
as it had meant to and vanished into the dark doorway
of the stable. Barney hurled himself forward, slammed
the lower half of the door shut and then the upper
half, and gasped: 'Quick, quick, quick, somebody bolt
it!' Lou and the Indian struggled with the bolts, and
at last they all sank down on the pavement feeling
exhausted and weak.

The other children had now opened the gates of the
yard and the rest of the party were streaming in, chattering and asking questions.

'Where's the leopard?'

'Have you caught the leopard?'

'Is the game over now?'

'What d'you mean it was a *real* leopard?'

'Let's have another leopard-hunt. It was super fun.'

'Why can't we have another leopard-hunt?'

'What d'you mean the leopard's in the stable?
There's the leopard!'

'*Two* leopards? Well that's not fair, nobody told us
there were two leopards.'

'Why can't we see the other leopard in the stable?
Let's let it out and have another hunt.'

And the boy in the Zorro suit was actually fumbling
with the bolts and trying to open the door of the stable.
Stig, who was standing there, rapped him over the
knuckles with the haft of his spear.

'All right, cave man!' said Zorro crossly. 'I can open the door if I want to. It's not your business!' But Stig turned his spear round and threatened him with the point, and Zorro retreated, saying: 'No need to get nasty!'

Then suddenly all the windows of the big house blazed with light again, and then the voice of Mrs Fawkham-Greene came from the front steps, calling: 'Children, children, you're all to come in *at once!* Everyone inside, as quick as *ever* you *can!*' She sounded as if she was almost frightened of something.

As they all trooped round to the front entrance they noticed a big truck in the drive, and strange men standing around, and some of the men had rifles! Mrs Fawkham-Greene was standing on the steps flapping her hands. 'Come along, come *along!*' she cried. 'It was so naughty of you to go outside. One, two, three, four, five . . . Just go in the hall and stand still while I count you all!' They stood wide-eyed in the hall as Mrs Fawkham-Greene slammed the big door behind her, leant against it with a white face, counted the guests and then counted again, and muttered to herself: 'Oh, dear, how many should there be? Little Jonathan couldn't come because of measles, and then there's Betty Strickwell didn't answer . . .'

The children began to join in with helpful voices:

'Where's the other cave man?'

'Yes, there's supposed to be two cave men, I saw them.'

'And there's two –'

'Please, please, be quiet, you only confuse me,' moaned Mrs Fawkham-Greene. She turned to a strange man in a raincoat who was standing by the door. 'I think they're all here, Mr Er,' she said. 'Would you like to explain?'

'Sorry to spoil your party, kiddies,' said the man. 'I'm from Bottom's Circus, and I'm afraid one of our animals got loose from its travelling cage and it must be somewhere about here. But don't worry, we'll soon catch him.'

There were excited gasps and whistles from the children. Then Lou spoke up.

'It was a leopard, wasn't it?' she said.

The man looked at Lou. 'Yes, girlie,' he smiled. 'Like you, only a bit fiercer.'

And Barney stepped forward. 'It's all right sir,' he said. 'We put it in the stables, me and Stig and Lou. I'll help you get it out if you like.'

8. Midsummer Night

BARNEY lay awake on his bed. It was hot, and he hung his feet over the edge of the bed to cool them down. Somewhere in the room a summer mosquito was whining about, and from outside came the drone of a farm tractor working late, and the barking of dogs from the village. Though the curtains were drawn he knew it was still daytime outside. It would be daytime for hours yet, but he had to go to bed in the daylight just because he was only eight. Still, he wouldn't go to sleep. He couldn't, it was so hot and stuffy.

He had asked his Grandmother why he couldn't stay up until it was dark and she had explained that today was the longest day and tonight was the shortest night, and that it wouldn't get dark until after ten o'clock, far too late for a boy of eight to stay up. All right, he thought, if it was the shortest night he wouldn't go to sleep at all. He would see what it was like *not* to sleep.

Barney thought of Stig. I bet he doesn't go to sleep when it's daylight, he thought. And he's – how old? How old *was* Stig? About eight? Eighty? Eight hundred? Eight thousand?

Thinking of figures made Barney feel drowsy and before he knew it he had gone off to sleep.

It was Grandmother going to bed that woke him up again. She only opened the bedroom door a little to see if he was all right, but suddenly he was wide awake. Bother! He'd been asleep after all. But he wouldn't do it again. He'd stay awake now.

He got out of bed and looked out of the window. At first he thought it was still daytime, but no, the light came from a big white moon in the south. And in the north there was still a bluish light as if the sun had not gone far out of sight behind the elm trees.

He wouldn't go back to bed. He'd go out in the moonlight. He'd go and see Stig! His heart was thumping as he thought of the idea. It was still very warm, so he slipped on a pair of shorts and nothing else, and crept carefully out of the bedroom and down the creaking stairs. He pulled at the stiff bolts of the front door, trying to make no noise, but Dinah the spaniel, who slept downstairs, must have heard him, for she gave a questioning bark.

'Be quiet, Dinah,' whispered Barney crossly. 'It's only me. If you don't shut up you'll spoil everything.'

At last he managed to undo the stiff bolts and the lock, and the door swung open. He went out into the shadow of the house, and then into the moonlight. Everything was very still. Suddenly he jumped as he heard his name called.

'Barney!'

It was Lou, looking down from her bedroom window.

'Barney, what are you *doing*?' Lou hissed.

'Just going out. Nothing to do with you,' answered Barney quietly.

'But it's the middle of the night!'

'I know. I don't care. It's light as day.'

'Golly, so it is,' said Lou. 'But where are you *going*, Barney?'

'I'm not going to tell you.'

'Oh, *please*, Barney. Don't go yet! Can't I come too?' Lou begged.

Barney looked at the dark shadows under the fruit trees and thought of how shadowy the pit would be. Perhaps it would be better with two.

'All right. You can be my bodyguard. Hurry up then!'

'Oh, thank you, Barney!' Lou's head disappeared from the window, and soon Barney heard the click of her door and the creak of the stairs. When she appeared at the front of the house she had Dinah with her.

'I thought I'd bring Dinah too,' she said. 'As an extra bodyguard. Where are we going, Barney?'

'I'm going to see Stig.'

Lou gasped. 'Really and truly, Barney?'

'Of course. You can come with me to the pit. But I'll have to ask him if he wants to see you.'

'All right, Barney,' said Lou, with wide-open eyes.

They set off together through the moonlit garden.

'The red roses look black in the moonlight,' said Lou.

'Do they?' said Barney. 'I can see as well in the moonlight as in the daytime. Come on!'

They went through the gate into the paddock. Flash, the old pony, was awake and cropping the dewy grass. He tossed his head and snorted in surprise when he saw them, then went back to his feeding. They crossed the paddock, Dinah running in rings along rabbit trails, and came to the edge of the copse. In spite of the strong moonlight and the faint glow in the north, it looked very dark under the trees. They stood still.

'Sh!' said Barney.

'What is it?' whispered Lou.

'Isn't it quiet?' whispered Barney.

It was so quiet that they could hear the chiming of a church clock from a long way away. One, two, three, four, five, six, seven, eight, nine, ten, eleven, twelve.

'Midnight!' breathed Lou.

They walked to the edge of the dark wood together. Then they stopped.

How different the moonlight made everything look! They seemed to be standing on the edge of a deep forest, pierced by shadowy glades, instead of the straggling copse they knew. Even Dinah, who usually took any excuse to go plunging into the thickets after rabbits, seemed to hesitate. Then she sniffed, the hair on the back of her neck rose up, and she barked. Barney felt the hair on his neck rising too. He jumped, as the pony came prancing up and snorted behind them, and stood looking with pricked ears in the same direction as Dinah.

Dinah barked again. Then, before their eyes, a great animal leapt into a patch of moonlight in the glade and stood there for a moment.

'It's a stag!' breathed Lou with astonishment.

'I know,' whispered Barney.

'But there *aren't* any stags here!' exclaimed Lou.

Dinah was the first to recover from her surprise, and she hurled herself into the glade and the stag bounded off into the wood with Dinah in pursuit. The pony snorted and blew behind them, and stood there with quivering nostrils.

It was then that the children went midsummer crazy. Without a word Lou grabbed the pony by the mane, Barney legged her up on the pony's back, Lou hoisted him up in front, and before they could stop to think they had cleared the fence and were galloping – straight for the edge of the pit!

The pit was there all right. The pony poised on the edge – then with a spring and a scramble which kept them too busy clinging with legs and hands to think what was happening, Flash was down and up the other side! What *had* happened? Instead of the great quarry there was a mere scratch in the ground. And now nothing was familiar. They expected every minute to come to the cornfield beyond the copse, but the thickets and glades stretched on and on. They were reaching the slope which should have led to the lane, and Flash slowed down a little, but from far ahead came Dinah's mad yelping and the crashing of undergrowth, and the pony needed no urging to pursue the hunt. And still no landmarks came in sight. No open fields, no hedges, no orchards, no farms, only hazel-thickets, beech-woods, and the chalky hillside. Without a rein to guide or restrain him, the pony went like the wind, his head well up, and Barney and Lou could only cling there with their bare legs and look with round eyes at the strange landscape.

'Barney!' gasped Lou, clinging to her brother more tightly than she had ever done before. 'We're dreaming all this really.'

'You may be. I'm not,' Barney shouted against the wind, and twined his fingers more deeply in the pony's mane.

They were galloping up a little valley between clumps of bramble and taller bushes. There was no sound of barking from Dinah. Suddenly there in the moonlight was the dog, lying stretched out on the turf right in front of them. The pony slowed and swerved, the children fell off, in a tangle of limbs, on to the soft turf that smelt of wild thyme, and the pony trotted off casually to get his breath back. Of the stag there was no sign.

Barney and Lou sorted themselves out. Lou tried to stand up, but her legs felt woolly after using them to cling on with for so long, so she sat down again.

'Well Dinah,' she said to the dog. 'Where's the stag, eh? Couldn't catch it, I suppose. Never mind, you're not a stag hound, are you? Eh, Dinah?'

Then she turned to Barney. 'Barney, if we're not dreaming all this, where are we?'

'Don't know,' replied Barney. 'Let's go on just a little bit more, and maybe we'll see.'

There was a line of beech trees at the top of the little valley and Barney felt there must be something the other side of them. He scrambled up the slope, went between the dark trunks and beyond them was – nothing!

It was like flying. Smooth turf sloped down steeply under his feet, and far below the land was spread out like a map.

'Lou,' he called. 'Look where we are!'

They realized they were standing on the edge of the North Downs, a place they knew well enough, and the moon made everything as clear as day. And yet the more they looked the stranger it was. There should have been pylons striding over the land carrying electric cables. There should have been squares of orchard, hop gardens, villages, and churches. There should have been cement works in the distance by the river – and where was the tall television mast with the red light on top? They could see nothing but forest and heath over the whole floor of the valley, and out of the night strange animal noises came up to them. And in all this stretch of empty land there were only two – no, three – points of light twinkling, to show that man was somewhere about.

The nearest light was only a little way along the side of the hills, and now they could hear human voices coming from it.

'It's a camp fire,' said Barney. 'Come on, let's go and see.'

'But it might be savages or something,' said Lou doubtfully.

'There aren't any savages in England.'

'There aren't any stags in this part of England, but we just saw one. And this doesn't seem to be England at all.'

'Well, it must be somewhere,' said Barney. 'Let's go and ask those people.'

'I think we ought to be careful,' said Lou. 'Let's creep up through the woods and have a look.'

They went back into the shadow of the beech woods and made their way as quietly as they could over last year's crackling leaves and husks.

'Keep to heel, Dinah!' whispered Lou. 'Barney, I wish we had a lead. Dinah might give us away.'

'I've got some string in my pocket, I think,' said Barney. He rummaged in his pockets and found a coil of hairy string he had taken from a runner-bean that seemed to have finished with it. They tied it to Dinah's collar and went cautiously on. Soon the sounds of the camp were quite near and they could see the red firelight flickering through the black beech trunks.

'Sounds as if they are having a party,' said Lou. 'Listen! Music!'

'That's not music,' said Barney.

'Well it's jazz or something. Or one of those skiffle groups.'

As they moved towards the firelight, keeping to the shadows, the noises were so loud that they did not have to worry about keeping quiet themselves. They reached the last beech tree of the wood, a giant with thick roots coiling into the chalky soil and broad boughs spreading out towards the slope on which the camp stood.

'What are you doing, Barney,' hissed Lou, as Barney started scrambling on to one of the spreading branches.

'I'm going to climb this tree so I can see,'

'So am I then.'

'What about Dinah? You can't bring her up.'

'I'll tie her up here,' said Lou. 'Lie down, Dinah! Be quiet! There's a good dog!'

They climbed from limb to limb of the great beech tree until they got to a thick bough that grew out straight towards the firelight. Barney sat astride it and inched himself along until he reached a fork, far out over the bushes and brambles that straggled along the edge of the wood.

They had a perfect view of the camp. Or was it a camp? There were beehive huts made of poles planted in the ground, tied together at the top and thatched with straw and rushes. In an open space there was quite a crowd of people gathered round the fire. None of them seemed to be wearing much more than Lou and Barney. All of them seemed to have a lot of wild black hair, except for a few grey and white heads. The older ones were sitting, lying, or squatting around, toddlers were tumbling or sleeping in the dust, boys and girls were chasing each other round the outside of the crowd or teasing fierce-looking dogs.

The noise that was something like music came mostly from a group in the middle of the crowd near the fire. There were four figures in the group. One was holding half the jawbone of a large animal and running another longer bone up and down the teeth, making a scratchy rhythm. Another had a hollow log which he was hitting with two wooden clubs. The third was the singer. He didn't seem to have much idea of a tune and the children couldn't understand the words, but it was quite clear what the song was about. One moment the singer was a deer, grazing peacefully and then looking anxiously about. Then he was a hunter, stalking his prey with spear poised. Then he was the deer fleeing, the hunter throwing his spear, the deer falling, the hunter carrying it back to camp. The crowd became as excited as the singer, and joined in with hand claps and cries.

But there was yet another sound which the listeners could not quite understand, a kind of BLOONG, BLUNG, BLONG, BLOONG, not always on one note as most of the singing was, and not really taking much notice of the rhythm of the log-drum and jawbone. It was as if someone who had never heard a tune was trying to play one for the first time with a tea-chest, string, and broomstick.

Then the bone-scraper in his excitement joined the singer in a little shuffle-dance and the children could see the fourth member of the band. On the ground was a large hollow animal skull with great curving horns. Tied between the horns were three or four lengths of string or gut, and a small dark figure was squatting by this simple harp, plucking at the strings BLUNG BLONG BLOONG BLUNG, and taking very little notice of anyone else.

In fact the song came to an end, the drummer gave the final thump to his log, the bones-scraper rattled to a stop, but the little harpist went on with his three notes as if he were the only musician in the world. Some of the crowd began to laugh and jeer at him as he played away, but it wasn't until someone threw a meat bone, catching him on the head with a clunk the children could hear in their tree, that the player looked up, as if surprised to see that he was not alone.

Barney nearly fell off his branch. 'It's Stig!' he almost shouted.

'Hush, Barney!' Lou hissed. 'You'll give us away!'

'But it *is* Stig,' said Barney excitedly. 'I said he was clever. He probably invented that thing he was playing music on. Where's he going now?' For the little figure Barney said was Stig was rather sulkily walking away from the camp fire towards the trees.

'He's coming this way,' whispered Lou. 'Barney, you're not to give us away!'

'Why not? He's my friend.'

'What about all the others? Who are they? You never said about them.'

'I don't know who they are. I never saw them before.'

'Well, we'd better be careful, Barney.'

'Oh, all right!'

But what gave them away was Dinah, tied up at the bottom of the tree. She had been quiet up to now, but when she heard Stig walking towards the wood she began to growl and then to give short sharp barks. On the edge of the bushes, Stig at once froze into stillness. Dinah went on barking, and some of the wild children playing on the outside of the crowd heard her too. The bolder ones ran to the edge of the wood, the little ones ran to their parents by the fire. Soon a number of alarmed elders, snatching up spears and clubs, were making for the woods and the sound of Dinah's bark.

Lou and Barney clung to their high branch like squirrels, not daring to move. They could see the strange people on the edge of the wood, wondering at the unusual sound of a spaniel's bark, then at last plucking up courage to advance into the darkness of the bushes and the beech forest, holding their weapons at the ready.

Dinah's barking became more and more frantic as she heard the rustling of bodies through the bushes all round and the crackling and snapping of footsteps. Under cover of the noise Barney whispered: 'Lou, we've got to escape.'

'How can we?' breathed Lou.

'Look where that bough goes!' Barney pointed in the moonlight. The limb they were on stuck out into nothingness, but one of its branches went across to another long limb, and this one stretched out and rubbed shoulders with another great beech tree. If they climbed over into the other tree, Barney thought they could escape.

'We can go across there,' he whispered. 'Come on, while they're making all this noise.'

Lou's face seemed to go pale. 'Oh, Barney, we can't! And they'll find Dinah anyhow.'

'I'm going to try. Then perhaps we can rescue Dinah.'

He inched himself backwards along the limb they were sitting on until he reached the branch that grew crosswise. When he came to it he wondered what to do. It was too thin to sit astride so he decided to hang underneath it like a sloth by his hands and legs. Upside down like this he crawled through the empty air between the two big limbs. By bending his head right back he had an upside-down view of the floor of the forest, patched with moonlight – and right beneath him was a wild hunter, the tip of his spear pointing skywards, but looking at the ground. Barney hung without moving until the man had passed on, then moved as quickly and as quietly as he could to where the branch passed over the other great limb. Here he got himself right way up on the bough again. His heart was thumping and his legs felt quivery, but at least he was safer for a little while.

But now he had to go outward to where the two trees shook hands high in the air. He worked his way forward. As he went the boughs became thinner and swayed more. At last he was where the trees met. Where the branches crossed their movement in the wind had rubbed a great dry scar, and nothing he could do would stop a loud creak coming from this rubbing-place every time he moved.

'I must get over on to the other tree,' he thought. As quickly as he dared he turned round so as to go backward down the new branch, let go the branch he had just come up and – CRACK!

It was a dead branch!

Barney fell through nothing, then struck a flat leafy branch below, slid outwards from this on to a lower one, crashed through and fell the last few feet on to the soft forest floor.

9. The Standing Stones

FOR a moment Barney's brain bounced back to the first time he had fallen down the chalk cliff and met Stig. Then he opened his eyes and saw, not the face of the cliff with daylight at the top, but the pattern of beech boughs through which the full moon looked down at him. Then there was a rustle of branches, and he could see Lou clambering down towards him. She fell off the last low bough and ran to where he was lying.

'Barney!' she was saying. 'Are you all right, Barney?'

He sat up. 'Course I'm all right,' he said. 'Bit

scratched, that's all. Why didn't you stay up there if you didn't want to be caught?'

'I thought you were hurt, or I would have,' said Lou, looking around anxiously. Shadowy figures were moving towards them through the wood. One of them, with tousled head, skin skirt, and flint spear, came into the moonlight patch. Lou drew away from it, but Barney knew who it was.

'Hullo Stig!' he said. 'What are you doing here?'

Stig's teeth flashed in the moonlight, and then he looked curiously at Lou.

'Oh, this is only my sister, Stig,' said Barney.

'Is this really Stig?' whispered Lou.

'Yes, of course,' said Barney. 'My friend Stig.'

'Oh,' said Lou. 'Er, good evening, Mr Stig.' Stig merely grinned again in a friendly way and said nothing.

'Doesn't he speak English?' whispered Lou.

'No,' replied Barney.

'What does he speak then? Latin or French?'

'Don't know,' said Barney. 'You might try 'em.'

Lou didn't seem to be able to remember anything suitable to say to a savage spearman in a moonlit wood, so she said nothing. Meanwhile other figures had appeared from the shadows and were standing round in a circle, watching them. Stig made a few strange sounds, and they lowered their weapons. Then an argument broke out, with a lot of waving of arms towards the camp and pointing of fingers at Barney and Lou. Finally Stig smiled at them, held out his two hands to them, and made ushering movements.

'I think we're invited to the party,' said Barney.

They moved off through the wood, in a silence that was broken by a barking and whining, and there in the dark was Dinah, jumping around on the end of her string. Lou ran up to her.

'Poor Dinah,' she said. 'Did we leave you in the dark then? It's all right Dinah, it's only Barney's friend Stig and the other nice gentlemen.' Dinah didn't seem at all too sure about the other nice gentlemen, and stood there growling in her throat, until Stig came up and said something, and she actually licked his hand.

'That's funny!' Lou whispered. 'Dinah seems to know Stig.'

'Well, why not? Probably meets him when she goes rabbiting,' said Barney. 'You know, in the old days. I mean, when things are usual.'

They were on a forest track now, so narrow that they had to go in single file and not talk. But soon they came out from the edge of the wood on to the bare top of the hill, and now the women and bigger children who had not dared go into the dark wood ran up to stare at them.

'I don't suppose they've ever seen anything like us,' Lou whispered.

Barney took a look at Lou in the bright moonlight. 'Well, I don't know,' he said.' You can't see yourself, Lou. You don't look much different from them, except your hair's fair.'

Lou felt her tangled hair and looked at her ripped shorts, then looked at Barney with his legs all smeared with green from the bark of the trees.

'You don't look very different yourself,' she said.

They were walking over the smooth turf towards the cluster of huts. The armed tribesmen were on each side of them, and it was difficult for them to feel sure whether they were prisoners or guests. As they came near the huts Lou said: 'I thought Stigs were cave-men.'

'So they are. My friend Stig is, anyway,' said Barney.

'What have they got huts for then?' asked Lou.

Barney thought for a moment as they passed the huts. They were not much more than shelters, a few long branches tied together at the tops, thatched with leaves and bracken. 'Perhaps they're cave-men on holiday,' he said.

There *was* a holiday feeling about the tribe. They were sitting round the fires, from which there came smells of roasting meat. The men were together in groups, the women were looking after the meat on the spits or holding sleeping babies. Barney looked at a group of boys who were rolling and wrestling on the ground and whispered, 'Do you think we'll be allowed to play with them?'

'Better not,' Lou whispered back. 'We'll have to say how-do-you-do to whoever's giving the party first anyhow.' She tried to comb her hair with her fingers, but Barney, after taking a few leaves and twigs out of his, decided it wasn't worth trying.

They passed into the circle of firelight, and the crowd, who had been talking among themselves quite quietly before, fell silent, and everyone was looking at them. They walked in silence round the edge of the circle. Barney heard a very small whisper from Lou: 'Remember when we were bridesmaid and page at the wedding?' He did remember, and the feeling was about the same as when they had walked into the church with the bride. But this time they were the most important people in the procession.

On the other side of the circle was a group of older men, and in the middle there was a figure sitting on a tree-trunk. As they went nearer they could see that he had white hair, very bright black eyes, and was dressed in some very silky fur, with necklaces and bangles of animals' teeth. They didn't need to be told that this was the chief. Barney felt the black eyes boring into him – and then suddenly all the rest of the party fell flat on the ground.

'Lou, what happened?' he whispered very small. 'They all fell down!' Then he saw that Lou was trying to curtsey, which looked a bit silly with bare legs and torn shorts, and he thought it might be good manners to bow. The chief, or King, or whoever he was, seemed satisfied with his touch-the-toes-bend and Lou's contortions, and a smile appeared on his face. In fact Barney thought he was going to laugh.

But then the chief looked stern again and barked a short question at Stig, who had now stood up again. It obviously meant: 'What on earth have you got there?'

And Stig began to speak. Barney was amazed. He thought of all the time he had spent with Stig, when they'd hardly said a word to each other, though they had understood each other well enough – and here he was making a speech like somebody on the wireless. It sounded wonderful, but he didn't understand a word of it.

'What's he saying?' whispered Lou.

'He's saying how we came here,' said Barney.

'Well how *did* we?' Lou whispered again.

'You know,' said Barney.

'I jolly well *don't* know,' said Lou, quite crossly. 'That's why I want to know what he's saying.'

It *would* be interesting, thought Barney, as the speech went on and on. At one point Stig would wave his spear towards the North Star, at another he would thump himself over the heart and slap Barney on the back.

'He's saying I'm his friend,' said Barney.

'A jolly good thing you are,' muttered Lou. Barney felt proud.

Stig stopped. There was a silence as the chief seemed to think for a while. Then he rose to his feet. He spoke in a strong, majestic voice, turning his head first to Lou and Barney, then to one side of the assembled tribe and then to the other. He raised his arms to the stars, waved his hand at the moon, placed both hands over his heart and then seemed to be blessing the children and the rest of the tribe.

'I think *he's* friendly too,' whispered Barney.

The chief had finished and there was silence again. Everyone seemed to be looking at Barney and Lou, and an awful thought came into Barney's mind.

'Lou,' he whispered in the silence. 'I think it's our turn to make a speech.'

'Well, go on then!' said Lou.

'I don't know the language!'

'I *thought* you didn't,' said Lou unkindly. 'Do it in English then!'

'I don't know what to say,' said Barney, quite sure that whatever happened, *he* wasn't going to make a speech. '*You* do it!'

'Why should I?'

'You're always good at talking. Go on!' said Barney. He could see that Lou wasn't sure whether to be pleased or not at this remark, but it felt as if the silence

had gone on for hours. Lou looked round desperately, took a deep breath, and started:

'Mister Chairman, Headmistress, Governors, Ladies and Gentlemen – golly that's not right, lucky you can't understand English! It is with great pleasure that I come here today to present the prizes at your speech day. Remember, girls, that schooldays are the happiest days of your life. We can't all win prizes but –

('Go on, Lou!' said Barney. 'That's jolly good!')

'– but, I come to bury Caesar not to praise him, the evil that men do lives after them, it droppeth like the gentle rain from heaven, upon the place beneath. Once more into the breach, dear friends, once more! Beware the jabberwock, my son, the jaws that bite, the claws that scratch, beware the jub-jub bird and shun the vorpal Tumtum tree – how does it go, Barney?

('You're doing jolly well, Lou!' exclaimed Barney. 'Poetry!')

'Christmas is coming!' said Lou, getting the hang of it and spreading out her arms to the audience. 'The geese are getting fat!' she declaimed, pointing at the moon. 'PLEASE!' she begged, holding out her hand, 'put a *penny*' – she paused – 'in the old man's hat,' she finished with her hand on her heart.

'That was super, Lou,' said Barney. 'I wish I'd done it now!'

'Well, you can next time,' said Lou, wiping her brow. But it seemed to have worked. The chief smiled at them and waved them to sit down near him. Then he looked at Dinah, standing rather unhappily beside Lou on the end of her string. He motioned to Lou to bring this strange tame animal to him, and Lou led the dog up and said: 'Shake hands with the nice chief, Dinah!'

Dinah didn't feel like raising a paw, but the chief gently stroked her back and ears, then ran his hand over the skin he was wearing and said something in his strange language.

'He's saying what a nice coat Dinah's got,' said Lou, pleased because she had brushed it such a lot.

'Probably saying what a nice coat it would make for

him,' said Barney, but Lou just said, 'Oh, Barney, *don't*,' and pulled Dinah to her side.

They sat at the side of the royal party and waited, and they had a strange feeling that everyone else was waiting too, waiting for something special. The tribesmen were just sitting around, talking in low voices, and sometimes everyone stopped talking altogether and just listened, and the chief seemed to have his eyes fixed on the mists at the bottom of the valley.

A man came from the back of the crowd, carrying two bull's horns, which he offered to Barney and Lou.

'What are we supposed to do with these?' Barney asked Lou. 'Blow them?'

Lou took one. 'Careful, Barney,' she said. 'There's something in them.' Barney took his. It was full of some liquid. They looked at the chief and the old men and saw that they were holding horns too. Then the chief lifted his to his mouth, drank what was in it at one swig, and threw the horn over his shoulder.

'It's to drink,' said Barney, and they both realized they were thirsty, and both took a deep swallow from the horns. Then they both made the same face. 'Eugh!' Lou spluttered. *'Beer!'*

Barney just threw his full horn over his shoulder. A rather fat sleepy tribesman sitting behind him got most of the beer in his face. He seemed surprised but didn't mind very much as he licked the drops running down his nose. Lou got rid of hers much more carefully.

Now the food was coming round. Men were standing near the fires taking the meat off the spits and cutting it up, and others came running with smoking joints which they handed first to the chief and then to the other important men and to the children. The smell had been delicious, but when they looked at the stringy blackened meat on the bones they had been handed, they didn't feel so hungry.

'D'you think it will be bad manners if we don't eat it?' Lou said doubtfully.

'Perhaps they don't have manners,' said Barney. 'It can't be good manners to throw your cup over your shoulder.'

'The chief did it, so it must be,' said Lou. 'You can't tell with manners.'

They looked at the chief again. He had gnawed the meat off his bone in no time, and now he flung it backwards to the rear of the crowd, where it was seized by one of the pack of wildish dogs that were waiting around.

'Oh well, that's easy,' said Lou. 'Here you are Dinah. Nice bone! With meat on!' Barney also handed his piece to the dog, and Dinah gnawed away happily like the rest of the tribe.

At last the champing jaws on all sides died away, fingers were wiped on the grass or in the hair, and the tribe settled down again with their air of waiting for something.

Barney, who was lying back on the soft turf, heard it first.

'What's that?' he exclaimed, sitting up suddenly.

'What's what?' Lou asked.

'Something in the ground,' said Barney. Now that he was sitting up he couldn't hear it. He lay down again and put his ear to the ground. The sound came again, a sort of thumping. He made Lou put her head to the ground, and for a time they heard nothing, and then the thump came again.

By now there was a shushing among the tribe, and some of them seemed to be hearing something too. Everyone became quite silent and after a time the sound could be heard through the air, as well as being a shake in the hillside. There was a long time between thumps – Barney counted up to twenty quite slowly, but they kept coming, and they seemed to be coming closer. It could have been the footsteps of some great giant or monster, plodding unhurriedly towards them out of the marshy valley. Barney looked at Lou, and he could see that she was thinking the same thing.

'What can it be, Lou?' he whispered.

'I don't know. Could be anything.'

'Could it be one of those brontosauruses?' But Lou hushed for silence, and then Barney too caught another sound that went with the thumps of the footsteps. Before each thump there was a sort of long-drawn wail, so that it sounded like 'eeeeyoooooo-THUMP ... eeeeyoooooOTHUMP' ... and each time the whole chalky hill shook until they could feel it in their bones, sitting on the springy turf.

Everyone had heard it now, even the chief and the old men, who Barney supposed might be a little deaf. The circle of tribesmen round the fire was breaking up, and everyone was moving towards the edge of the steep slope that plunged down to the valley.

'Come on!' said Barney. 'We've got to see what it is!' They got up and ran with the others.

At the bottom of the valley the forest stretched away

to the distant hills under the moonlight, and blankets of low mist lay with the trees poking their heads through them. They strained their eyes to see through the mist where the sounds seemed to be coming from, then Lou gasped and clutched Barney's arm and pointed.

'Look!' she breathed. 'There it is!'

Barney saw it almost at the same moment, though he still didn't know what it was he saw. Out of the mist at the base of the hill, there heaved itself every now and then a dark shape that stood up for a moment and then each time fell forward in their direction. And every time it appeared there came this wail, followed by the earth-shaking thump. And now there seemed to be an extra sound attached to it, between the wail and the thump, like this: eeeeyooooooough-THUMP ... eeeeyooooooughTHUMP ... eeeeyoooough-THUMP – and the sound seemed to be not one loud voice, but many voices – and then Barney could see that the dark shape had sort of strings or feelers joined to it. Dinah, standing between them, had seen it now, and the hair was standing up on her neck and back, and Barney felt that his was too.

Still watching, fascinated, Lou said, 'Barney, we're dreaming all this of course. I'm going to pinch myself and then I'll wake up.'

'Don't you dare wake up and leave me here!' said Barney.

'Well, you pinch yourself at the same time,' said Lou. They pinched themselves. Nothing happened.

'Are you awake?' Barney asked.

'No,' replied Lou.

'I know what,' said Barney. 'I'll pinch you.' He pinched Lou and she squealed.

'You don't have to do it so hard!' she said. 'Perhaps it's your dream and not mine. My turn to pinch you.' She pinched him.

'You beast, Lou, that hurt!' said Barney. 'Look, we can't both be dreaming the same dream, so we must be both awake. I wish we weren't.' He took his eyes off the Thing and turned to someone standing next to him. It was Stig.

'Stig, thank goodness you're here!' gasped Barney. 'What is it, and what's going to happen?'

Stig just looked at him in his usual not-understanding way. But he grinned, and he really seemed quite cheerful and not at all worried!

'Lou, here's Stig,' said Barney. 'He seems to think it's all right.'

'Does he?' said Lou, looking round. 'Well, perhaps it's a tame Thing. Or a Usual Thing, anyhow.'

They felt better with Stig standing so cheerfully be-beside them, but Dinah suddenly decided that it was a Thing she didn't like at all, turned tail, jerked the string from Lou's hand, and bolted, with Lou after her shouting: 'Dinah, Dinah, come back! *Nice* Thing, Dinah! *Dinah-come-here!*' And at the same time Stig made a come-on wave to Barney and some of the other men and started down the steep slope. Barney found himself running with him, panting, 'I'm coming, Stig, wait for me. Stig, Stig, wait! You haven't got your spear, Stig!' – for he only just noticed that neither Stig nor the other men had brought their weapons with them.

But now that he had started running down the hill-side he knew he couldn't possibly stop, and he would be upon the Thing before he had time to wonder any more what it was.

This mist was the sort that wasn't there when you got to it, but spread the moonlight around like daylight, and Barney was still running down the last bit of hill

when he could see quite plainly what it all was – the dark shape, the strings, the wail and the grunt and the THUMP!

On the track leading along the base of the hill was a crowd of tribesmen. They were divided into two groups. Those nearer to him were pulling on ropes, those further away were working long poles, and the thing they were man-handling was a great rough slab of dark rock, at least twice as high as the tallest man.

And this was the way they were heaving it along: The slab of rock was lying flat on the ground. Twelve men with pointed stakes pushed them under the edge of the rock and levered it about a foot off the ground. A much larger group of men pushed much longer poles under the rock as far as they would go, and lifted it still higher by pushing upwards on the poles. To the top ends of these poles, long ropes of twisted hide had been tied, which passed over the top of the rock to the men in front. When the rock was high enough, the men in front pulled all together on the ropes, the rock rose until it was standing upright, seemed to stop there for a second, and then fell forward with the mighty THUMP that they had heard on the top of the hill. And the voice of the monster was the heave-ho of the men as they heaved together on the levers and ropes, and grunted together at the difficult point when the rock was half-way to standing up.

Barney was almost disappointed at the disappearance of the monster, but there was no time to stand around. The job was now to get the rock up the hill, and all the new helpers from the camp were needed. Without a pause in the slow footsteps of the rock they joined in the work – or rather it was like joining in a game or a dance. Barney grabbed the end of a rope, behind Stig, and watched what he did. They faced the stone, and had to walk towards it while the men the other side lifted the poles back to fit them again under the rock. Then they had to take up the slack, but not pull until the rock was lifted to the half-way mark.

Then all together, with the men on the other two ropes, they had to take the strain, heave on the rope until the rock was standing upright, and then heave no more, because it was no use pulling the rock over towards them, it could fall by itself.

Barney soon found it tiring, and wondered how long they could keep going like that. He started to say, 'Wouldn't it be better if –?' but as soon as he started talking Stig trod on his toe and then the rope was jerked through his hand as they lifted the poles back for the next heave. He noticed then that nobody was making suggestions, nobody was arguing, nobody was even giving orders. They just sang their wailing song: 'Eeeeyoooooough!' pulled together, walked up a few steps together, rested together while the pole-pushers worked – and Barney began to see that they could keep this up for hundreds of miles. And they probably *had*, because he couldn't think where they could find slabs of rock like this anywhere near.

Of course they couldn't go straight up the hill. It was too steep. But there was a grassy track slanting along the hillside, and up it they slowly humped the great rock.

They were getting near the camp now, and the women and children ran out to meet them and shout encouragement. Barney heard a voice he recognized, and turned his head and saw Lou among them, holding an excited Dinah. 'What are you going to do with it, Barney?' she was saying. 'I can't help 'cause I can't leave Dinah.' But as soon as he paid attention to what Lou was saying he got trodden on and jerked again, so he gave up trying to hear what she was shouting.

He thought he heard her say, 'Wouldn't it be better if you had wheels . . .', but there didn't seem to be much he could do about it.

Now, although it was the steepest part of the track, they seemed to be going quicker. Barney had the feeling of being at the end of a race, and making the final sprint. He looked round, and saw the chief standing there alongside the track. Then he thought of Lou's question, and for the first time wondered what they *were* going to do with this lump of rock. He supposed it was some kind of present for the chief. He hoped he would like it.

With a last couple of quick heaves, they laid the rock almost at the feet of the king, one man said something short in a loud voice, and all the rope-men and pole-men fell on their faces towards the king. Barney did too, this time. He was too tired to do anything else.

The king raised his arm. More speeches, Barney thought. But no, it seemed that the job was not finished.

He sat up and saw that leading away from where the rock lay was a sort of raised mound. This end of it was level with the ground but the far end ran out to the tops of three other huge stones that were standing upright lower down the hillside. Barney thought he could see, now, what they had brought the slab all the way up the hill for. If they humped it along this mound, they could put it so that it rested on top of the three standing stones. And there it would be – a house for the king, or a temple, or whatever it was that people put big stones across the top of others for. It seemed a grand idea to Barney.

He could see now that it wasn't going to be the same as bringing it along the track. Now it was going *down hill*. If they weren't careful it could go bounding away down the slope and even knock the standing stones flying like a lot of skittles.

The old king stood speaking to the group of important men. He seemed to be pointing to the eastern sky with one hand and urging them on with the other. Barney looked towards where the king was pointing. Was the sky beginning to get light? Was it nearly morning? Was there something that had to be done before the night came to an end? – before the end of the shortest night! the night that seemed to have been going on for such a long time?

The women and children scrambled down the hill to get a good view of the standing stones, and there was a lot of scolding and cuffing of little ones who got themselves in the way of where the stone was to come. The men with the poles and ropes made ready again. This time it was different: because of the steepness of the slope they couldn't pull from the front, but had to do all the lifting and pushing from behind. And to stop the stone running away down the hill there was a rope leading up-hill behind it, with a lot of people hanging on it to act as a brake. Stig took hold near the end of this, and Barney attached himself last of all, as anchor-man.

There was no hearty heave-ho-ing this time. It was easy enough to lift the rock on edge, but then everybody watched anxiously as the brake-rope was paid out and the rock was allowed to sink gently forward. There was no loud thump either, but a lot of hissing of breath and sighs of relief as each turn-over was safely done.

The steps along the top of the mound towards the top of the standing stones were even more anxious. One mistake, and the stone could topple sideways off the mound and charge off down-hill. Barney thought the women and children were standing dangerously close on each side. But they made six steps safely along the mound, each time letting the stone settle gently down by the brake-rope. And now it was standing on its edge near the end of the mound, ready to be lowered on to the top of the standing stones. The king was looking anxiously at the sky, which now showed a bright glow over the shoulder of the downs to the East. Sunrise couldn't be far off. The workers on the brake-rope took the strain as the stone began to fall forward.

But what was this?

Dinah, of all things, scrambling up the mound straight in front of the toppling stone, with Lou in desperate pursuit! And then Lou's voice shouting, 'Stop! Stop! Don't let it down! There's a baby!' and there was Lou disappearing in front of the stone too!

The stone was moving. Everyone on the brake-rope was doing his best to hold it back, but once it had started it was almost impossible. Barney, on the end, dug his heels into the slippery turf, but he could feel himself being dragged slowly forward.

And then he saw, just beside him on the hillside, a scrubby thorn tree, weather-beaten and stunted, but with strong roots clutching the earth.

'Stig!' he gasped. 'The tree!' Stig looked round and saw. With one hairy arm Stig reached out and grabbed the trunk of the tree. The rope was wrapped around his other wrist and his bones seemed to crackle as his arms took the strain – but the brake-rope stopped moving forward. Trying not to fumble, Barney passed the end of the rope twice round the little tree and pulled it taut, and Stig grinned as he saw that he could let go. The hide rope stretched, the roots of the tree strained in the ground, but Barney let himself look at the stone, and saw that it was not moving. And then Lou appeared from under the tilted stone, followed by Dinah, and carrying a naked, black-haired Stig-baby.

The king shouted impatiently. Barney let the end of the rope run out round the tree-trunk, the great slab fell forward with a hollow sound on to the tops of the standing stones and . . .

*

. . . and over the shoulder of the downs appeared a red spark, and the valley was flooded with light. It was sunrise. From the low mist in the bottom of the valley appeared the spire of a church, the tops of oast houses and electricity pylons. The solid forest was gone, and there were the squares of cornfield, orchard, and hop-garden. There were the villages, and the distant chimneys of cement-works, and the broad ribbon of the main road sweeping down the hill below.

Barney looked round the hillside. The people of the tribe had disappeared. There were no huts, no sign of a camp fire. They had all vanished with the last shades of darkness. But one thing had not changed. The three stones with the great slab on top were still before his eyes – weathered now, with grey lichen growing on them. The mound was not there, but the stones stood just as they had done when he had let go the last of the rope. Sitting against them was Lou, blinking her eyes at the rising sun as if she was waking from a deep sleep, and holding Dinah in her arms.

'Oh, Barney, I've had such a funny dream,' said Lou sleepily. 'I'm glad I've woken up, though.'

'So did I,' said Barney.' Are you sure we've woken up?'

Lou looked round. 'Well, I dreamt about a tribe of people long ago,' she said. 'They've all gone and now it's *now*. So it must have been a dream.'

'What are we doing here then?' asked Barney.

Lou opened her eyes at that. 'Good gracious,' she said. 'We don't usually wake up on top of a hill, do we?' She curled herself up at the foot of the stone and shut her eyes. 'I'm going to dream myself back to bed,' she said firmly.

Barney shook her. 'Get up, Lou!' he said. 'It isn't that sort of a dream at all. We really are here. We've got to get back to Granny's somehow.' Barney knew that it was something more than a dream. The tiredness in his arms and legs told him that he really had been hauling the great stone that looked as if it had been there for thousands of years.

He walked round to the front of the stones, where the open side looked over the valley – and there, sitting in the entrance as if he was on his own front porch, was Stig.

Barney gaped and Stig grinned. Lou put her head round the stone and gasped too. 'Stig!' she exclaimed. 'What are you doing here? If you're a midsummer fairy, or whatever the others were, you're supposed to vanish too.'

'But I told you,' said Barney. 'Stig's always here. He's my friend.'

*

Barney and Lou have almost forgotten how they got back to the house that summer morning. They re-

member catching the pony, who was grazing peacefully on the hilltop, and riding back half-asleep, clitter-clatter through the empty lanes, with Stig walking beside them. And they remember falling into their beds, and waking very late on Midsummer Day. Probably they agreed on the way back not to say anything about what had happened. Anyhow, what could they say?

It wasn't until quite a long time later that they went with their parents for a picnic on the North Downs where the four stones stand. And as they ate their sandwiches their parents got into an argument about stone-ages and bronze-ages, and about how the stones had got there at all, until Barney said, without thinking, 'They had *flint* spears, and it was the heave-ho that did it.'

And everybody thought about this quite a lot, and had to admit that Barney was probably right, though they couldn't think how he knew.

And then Barney and Lou said together, 'But I wonder how the baby got there?' And that was a question nobody could answer.

And what about Stig? Well, if you ask Barney he will say in an off-hand manner that he's still living in the dump. The grown-ups never really knew just how real he was, but they got used to the idea that wherever there was a pile of old thrown-away things an unseen Stig was likely to be poking around in it. And whenever there was a particularly odd job to be done (like making sure a rainwater butt didn't spring a leak when it was empty and overflow when it was full – or a new tool for lifting parsnips) then someone would say: 'Let's get Stig to fix it!'

Actually the dump's filling up fast now, and Stig may be on the move. One report was that he'd been seen working at a garage by the main road, where they collect old wrecked cars and put the pieces in rusty piles. And somebody else said he saw him in a back lane of that woody country at the top of the Downs, mending a chicken-run with an old wire mattress. It certainly sounded like Barney's friend Stig, but perhaps it was only a relative of his.

It all started with a Scarecrow.

Puffin is seventy years old.
Sounds ancient, doesn't it? But Puffin has never been
so lively. We're always on the lookout for the next big
idea, which is how it began all those years ago.

Penguin Books was a big idea from the mind of
a man called Allen Lane, who in 1935 invented
the quality paperback and changed the world.
**And from great Penguins, great Puffins grew,
changing the face of children's books forever.**

The first four Puffin Picture Books were hatched in 1940 and the
first Puffin story book featured a man with broomstick arms called
Worzel Gummidge. In 1967 Kaye Webb, Puffin Editor, started the
Puffin Club, promising to 'make children into readers'.
She kept that promise and over 200,000 children became
devoted Puffineers through their quarterly instalments of
Puffin Post, which is now back for a new generation.

Many years from now, we hope you'll look back and
remember Puffin with a smile. **No matter what your age
or what you're into, there's a Puffin for everyone.**
The possibilities are endless, but one thing is for sure:
whether it's a picture book or a paperback, a sticker book
or a hardback, **if it's got that little Puffin
on it – it's bound to be good.**